I0609059

Charles Reade, Hugh Walpole, Herbert Van Thal

Autobiography of a Thief and Jack of all Trades

A Matter-of-Fact Romance

Charles Reade, Hugh Walpole, Herbert Van Thal

Autobiography of a Thief and Jack of all Trades
A Matter-of-Fact Romance

ISBN/EAN: 9783337376734

Printed in Europe, USA, Canada, Australia, Japan

Cover: Foto ©Raphael Reischuk / pixelio.de

More available books at **www.hansebooks.com**

AUTOBIOGRAPHY OF A THIEF

AND

JACK OF ALL TRADES,

A Matter=of=Fact Romance.

BY

CHARLES READE,

AUTHOR OF "IT IS NEVER TOO LATE TO MEND."

LONDON:

WARD, LOCK, AND TYLER,

WARWICK HOUSE, PATERNOSTER ROW

AUTOBIOGRAPHY OF A THIEF.

THE readers of 'It is never too late to mend' may remember that in vol. ii. the chaplain set the thief to write his life honestly. He was not to whitewash, and then gild himself, nor yet to vent one long self-deceiving howl of general, and therefore sham penitence, but he was to be, with God's help, his own historian and sober critic. Accordingly Thomas Robinson wrote this autobiography in —— gaol: and my readers may have noticed that at first I intended to print it with the novel.

It cost me a struggle to resign this intention; for it was the central gem of my little coronet. But the novel, without the autobiography, was five ordinary volumes by printers' calculation, and a story within a story is a frightful flaw in art.

Moreover, I was attacking settled, long-standing prejudices. Prejudice is a giant, against whom Truth and Humanity need to be defended with great spirit, and, in some desperate cases, with a tiger-like ferocity: 'À dur âne dur aiguillon :' but there must be some judgment too; and, take my word for it, there always has been *some* judgment used, wherever so hard a battle is won. I feared then to multiply paradoxes, and to draw once too often on the faith of the public, as well as on its good heart, I, who carried no personal weight with me.

But I think my readers are now ripe for this strange but true story, and I dedicate it in particular to such as will deign to accept this clue to my method in writing—

I feign probabilities; I record improbabilities: the former are conjectures, the latter truths: mixed they make a thing not so true as Gospel nor so false as History : viz., Fiction.

When I startle you most, think twice before you disbelieve me. What able deceiver aims at shocking credulity? Distrust rather my oily probabilities. They should be true too if I could make them; but I can't: they are guesses.

You have seen Thomas Robinson, alias Hic, alias Ille, alias Iste, tinted in water-colours by me : now see him painted in oils by himself, and retouched by Mr. Eden.

A thief is a man: and a man's life is like those geographical fragments children learn ' the contagious countries' by. The pieces are a puzzle : but put them together carefully and lo ! they are a map.

The thief then mapped his puzzle; and I think his work will stand.

These caged autobiographers have a great advantage as writers over other autobiographers that sing false notes of egotism in

London squares, and American villas built ære
alieno.

Carceravis has been publicly convicted.
Mavis and Philomele have not met with so
much justice. They could eclipse the novelist
and the historian ; but they don't even rival
them. An alternative lies before them : to
chronicle themselves and their acts, and so
add great instructive pictures of man to the
immortal part of literature, or to idealize, as
our pedants call it, to slur, falsify, colour themselves up here and tone themselves down there.
Unfortunately for letters they invariably choose
the liedeal : and instead of coming out bright
as stars, the interesting, curious, instructive,
valuable, rogues, humbugs, and courtesans
they are, and so being the darlings of pos-
terity, they go mincing to trunkerity, tame
negative insipid characterless creatures, not
good enough for an example, not bad enough
for a warning, but excellent lining for a bandbox.

No. It is to the detected part of the community we must look for an honest autobiography. Not that self-deception ever retires wholly from a human heart, but that in these there is no good opinion of the world to back their self-deception. It is not so with many an unconvicted rogue, who is far below an average felon: the banker who steals not from strangers but friends; steals from those who have a claim to his gratitude as well as his honesty: the rector who preaches Christ, and swindles the young curate out of every halfpenny contrary to law, because the poor boy must get a title though he buy it and begin life with debt: how will he end it? The anonymous assassin, the cowardly caitiff of a scribbler who, with no temptation but mere envy, stabs the great in the dark and truckles to them face to face. A felon is a man, and often a resolute one; but what is this thing that stabs and runs away into a hole? the shopkeeping assassin who puts red-lead (a deadly poison) into red pepper, and sells death to those by whom he lives.

The shopkeeping assassin who puts copper, a deadly and cumulative poison, into pickles and preserves; and poisons those by whom he lives. The English assassin who poisons the young children wholesale in their sugar-plums, and then reads with virtuous indignation of the sepoys who bayoneted them in their rage instead of killing them cannily.

The miller, abandoned of God, and awaiting here on earth his eternal damnation, who, king of all these Borgias, thief and murderer at once, poisons young and old at life's fountain, breaks life's very staff, mixes plaster of Paris with the flour that is the food of all men, the only food, alas, of more than half the world.

These and a score more respectables are the hopeless cases. A cracksman, or a swell mobsman is terribly hard to cure. But these are incurable. The world's good opinion fortifies their delusion. They open their eyes for the first time in hell. A pickpocket now and then opens them in gaol.

We owe to —— gaol this slippery one who paints himself a slipperyish one, and does not falsify as well as filch.

It is important to observe that this is the man's history not after the events recorded in the novel, but before. His foundation, not his roof. On this autobiographer the benign influences of religion, the solidifying effect of property, and the guardianship of a shrewd but honest wife, have since been be-stowed by heaven.

Add then this autobiography to his cha-racter as drawn by me in the novel, and you possess the whole portrait: and now it will be for you to judge whether for once we have taken a character that exists on a. large scale in Nature, and added it to Fiction, or, here too, have printed a shadow, and called it a man.

AUTOBIOGRAPHY.

I DID nothing that I particularly remember until I was fifteen, except learn my lessons with now and then a fight. I lived with my mother in Edinburgh. One day a person of gentlemanly appearance met a band of us as we were going to school, and inquired for me by name. He took me aside into a tavern, and after treating me, revealed himself to me as my father. He also gave me a crown, and promised to see me again but was unfortunately prevented, or perhaps forgot.

My education being now considered complete, I went to receive lessons in anatomy, at which I remained for the space of nine months.

I now formed an acquaintance with a young lady (At this time I was staying with my godfather upon my mother's decease.) But she was unfortunately a Romanist, and on this account my godfather ordered me to leave off her acquaintance, which I refusing, he ordered me out of the house. I complied with this harsh mandate, but first collected (A.) all the money I could find, which amounted to about £50—and with this I went to Dunfermline, and from there to the Rumbling Brigg, where I lodged with a couple well to do: I paid my board while my money lasted—but being now empty, and my host finding I was a scholar, I agreed to give him three lessons a day upon the sly, for which he privately contracted to give me secretly the money to pay his wife my board.

This lasted three months: but one evening as we were at our studies, and having neglected to lock the door, being become too bold by past impunity, the wife, who had discovered our retreat, having listened a moment or two, burst suddenly in upon us and falling (B.) on her knees exclaimed—

'Good heavens, am I married to a man who does not know that three times five make fifteen?' and burst into a flood of tears and reproaches.

This was the line of the table he was unfortunately repeating to me at the time.

His wife's conduct raising a counter-excitement in my pupil, and finding I had lighted a flame which would not easily be extinguished, I thought proper to retire and go back to Dunfermline.   Here I learned my first trade of the many I have practised.

I engaged myself to a master weaver and petty manufacturer.   Besides learning to take drafts of patterns, &c., I used to cast his accounts : but one day he sent me to the bank to draw some money : on this I absconded with the money and went to Edinburgh.

He pursued me so closely, that with the aid of the police he apprehended me before I had time to spend it   to avoid punishment I gave him back the money all but seventeen shillings, and he, who was a good-natured man, wished me to go back to my place ; but having borne a good name in the place until then, I thought shame to go back ; so I went to Newcastle after borrowing of my (C.) late master 15s. for the journey.

At Newcastle I went into a chemist's shop for some cough-lozenges : now it happened that a woman in the shop asked for some medicine. I forget just now what it was, but the shopboy took down the wrong : he took down a bottle containing camomile, I remember that —so I told the boy that he mistook the Latin term ; this naturally attracted the master's attention, and he looked up and saw I was correct ; so then he asked me several questions, and finding me fit for his purpose he took me into his service—and here for a long while all my sorrows were at an end : for I took a delight in studying my master's interests, and laying up knowledge.

He favoured me with his instructions, and

I enjoyed at times the company of his daughter, which was to me a comfort above all, and with whom I felt myself soon deep in love, and with her I spent many a happy hour after the business of the day was over, walking out in the evenings, while the moon with her bright and gentle rays gave to all things a delightful appearance, and seemed to lift up our minds to something above the grovelling cares of Time—or we heard the plaintive notes of the nightingale breaking the silence of the night, and calling us to join him in his songs of praise to the God of Nature. But sweeter still than the voice of the nightingale was the voice of my companion, which was sweetest of all when its topic (D.) would run to that portion, which forms the golden part of Cupid's dart.

In these innocent joys I spent four years.

But one unfortunate evening, having a drop too much at the time, I met Miss B. as usual, and opportunity and temptation unfortunately occurring, I was guilty of a felony that has always remained on my conscience more than any of those acts I have been guilty of, which the law describes to be the highest crimes.

From that night our walks beneath the moon by the river-side were no longer innocent, and we were no longer happy.

Oh (E.) cursed night and place that robbed a virgin of her purity! and oh cursed Tyne, why did not thou overflow thy banks and drive me away?—if now thy fountain-spring was to pour out streams of flaming lava it would not purge the disgrace out of thy dark banks—nay, if thy banks themselves were to become gold they would not ransom the character lost on that night nor restore the rest and quiet that now fled from my pillow.

Four months had scarce elapsed before I learned that consequences of a serious kind were to be expected.

I was in great perplexity : at last taking a

desperate course I with much hesitation asked my master for his daughter's hand.

My master, who though a good-natured was a hasty man, turned black and red at the idea, but recovering himself soon he turned it off as a jest—I saw by this that he would never consent, and dreading discovery I got a friend of mine to write to me (F.) from Edinburgh that my sister lay at the point of death and begged to see me.

Showing this letter to my master, I got leave of absence and a present for the journey, with which I started, promising to return in a week, but with no such intention.

I arrived at Edinburgh, and found my sister, whom I had spoken of as dying, just on the eve of marriage. I was at the wedding, but the nuptial feast was no feast to me, for it only recalled the thoughts of my own guilt.

I now began the world again.

I went to Stirling and obtained a situation

with a baker : but the work was much too hard for me, so I left him in two days, and took (A.) with me three pound ten shillings ; was apprehended in Glasgow and got sixty days.

On receiving my liberty I enlisted in Her Majesty's service and was marched on board the " Pique " frigate bound for the West Indies.

Here I remained until we got to Plymouth, where I made my escape, but was retaken in the town and brought back to the ship and put in irons on the spar-deck under cover of a tarpaulin—this was my prison till we reached St. Vincent : we anchored here for two days, and in the confusion of getting under weigh again I watched my opportunity, and having broken my padlock the day before, I stole into the captain's cabin, he being on deck, and took away a suit of his clothes, and dropped into the water ; and the weather being calm, and I being an excellent swimmer,

I swam alongside a brigantine that lay at anchor in the bay, and hailing her from the surface of the water, sang out—'Hallo! are you short of hands?'

'We are,' was the reply, 'where do you hail from?'

'What has that to do with it?' said I. So they hauled me on board.

The master, finding I had been educated, sent me on shore to his brother who kept a store; and so now I was his shopman.

I lived with my new master: we used to come to the shop in the morning and go home at night. We lived a mile and a half out of the town in a pretty Gothic house, which stood in the middle of a delightful garden bordered by sugar-canes—in front of the house was an avenue of orange and lemon-trees mixed: their branches bent with the exuberance of the fruit; and the ground glittered with great shaddocks and limes, that lay like lumps of gold, unheeded and rotting for abundance.

The air too was filled with the scent of thousands of rich flowers that were scattered about,
some by Nature, some by the hand of man—
in short it was an earthly paradise, in which I
might have ended my days if the demon of
change had not filled my mind with the desire
to behold once more my native country—
stupid fool.

I set sail, and after a stormy passage reached
the port of London.

I lodged in the Commercial Road till my
money was nearly gone, and then I became
disconsolate.

Wandering one day in the Ratcliffe High-
way it was my luck to fall in with an old
acquaintance, whom I had known through
being in trouble together; he introduced me
to a lodging-house keeper in the neighbourhood, who after a few words with my companion told me 'it was all right, we should
find means of settling.'

I went to bed, and when I wanted to get

up, my clothes were stolen, with the few shillings I had left. Remonstrating with the landlord, he said, 'Oh it is a mistake,' and disappearing for a few minutes, during which I heard high words and a bit of a tussle, he returned with my clothes and money

The next day seeing me very dull, and concluding by that I was ripe for business, he inquired the cause of my uneasiness.

I told him my last shilling was melting.

He laughed at this cause of trouble.

'You don't know' said he—'you are in the Mint.'

'In the Mint?' said I.

'Yes!' was his reply; 'in the Mint, my boy;' and with that he took up a chisel and went to the chimney and carefully removed a loose brick, and took out of the gap a tin box: he opened the box, and coins of every sort in profusion flashed upon my bewildered eyes—and not only coins, but dies and metal of all sorts for making them.

'Now,' said Crœsus, 'having gone so far you must take the oath at once.'

Four men, and four females were then summoned, and standing in the middle of them I took a solemn oath to this effect :—

> ' I hereby swear never to tell any one
> ' how to make " shoffle " nor where I
> ' learned it, nor yet to use any kind of
> ' language that may lead to the same,
> ' upon pain of death.'

Here followed imprecations upon my eyes and limbs, if broken, such as are used among freemasons, &c., but not being fit for your reverence's ears, I suppress that part.

The next process was to go and change a base sovereign, which I did accordingly, returning with nineteen and sixpence, and of which sixpence went for the gin.

Behold me now a shoffle-pitcher. But it was never my way to remain at the bottom of any business that I found worth studying. I therefore in the course of six months learned

to coin first a shilling, then a sovereign, then
the most difficult of all, a crown; and last of
all to make the moulds for each of these
coins, and as soon as I found I could make
a mould for a crown, I dissolved partnership, and went to Gravesend on my own
bottom.

Your reverence will blame me less for this
revolt if I tell you the terms on which we
worked with him whom I have called Crœsus,
and his name did begin with a C.

He had the half of every coin we uttered—
he had the cost of the metal besides, and the
half of every article purchased in the process
of uttering.

Now this was not fair: at least I think not,
because he did not share the risk.

I pitched on my own account about a
month; then finding the trade stale, and
having once or twice narrowly missed being
apprehended, I returned to London and be-
took myself to the diligent study of house-

breaking. I learned from a master how to make false keys—and having money by me and courting the company of the best cracksmen, and listening to all they said with respect and attention, I attracted notice, and was made a member of the body, and soon after permitted to take part in a job. It was a doctor's shop in the Commercial Road, and my share came to £50. And this was only the first of many transactions of the kind.

And as it becomes every one that is in a business to master it if possible, I will tell your reverence how I attended to mine, trusting you will not make it generally public, as it is not considered honourable among us to reveal the secrets of business, but only on account of your goodness I am willing to put you on your guard, and also your own friends —that is to say, such of them as have got anything to lose: but hope it will go no farther than the gaol.

Now as the chief work of practitioners in

our line is to find out where the money or valuables are kept, this was my plan :—

If it was a shop, I would go in and buy something, give the shopman a sovereign, and notice where he put it, and from whence he took the change, and at the same time how the door was fastened, whether with a lock or bar, or while my pal (for we always went in pairs) was engaging the shopman, I would take the dimensions of the same.

Or if it was a dwelling-house I would go and present the mistress with a card stating I was a china or glass-mender, a French-polisher, a teacher of music or dancing; and try every move to get admittance into the parlour, and then you may be sure my eyes were not shut.

Or else I would go and offer the servant some article for sale as a hawker, and would chaff and flatter her, and so perhaps get a notion where the plate was kept, and the next week come and fetch it away.

In the course of a few weeks I had collected somewhere about one hundred pounds in money and valuables, and finding the police had scent of me, I left London and went down by the Leith smack to Edinburgh.

Here I visited my friends and passed myself off in their society for a thriving tradesman.

I also sent some money to Miss B.—not that money could repay the injury I had done her, but still it would make her friends more civil to see that she wanted for nothing.

If my real character had not got wind in Newcastle I think at this time they would have let me marry her, and I think, bad as I am, I should have mended for her sake, for she was the only woman I ever really loved. (G.)

It is an old saying that 'the money which comes by the wind goes by the water.'

I have made thousands but never could keep as much as a £5 note.

In about a month nearly all my money was melted, and I set out on a cruise again.

Falling into some of my old haunts in Yorkshire I met with a friend who manufactured base coin, and, having passed a quantity of this and being now at my ease, I determined to study a new profession.

I therefore secluded myself from all my idle companions, took a quiet lodging, bought several medical books, and studied the human frame and the disorders to which it is subject.

I studied night and day with the same diligence I had given to coining, house-breaking, and my other professions.

In about a month I considered myself fit to start, which I accordingly did with as much pomp as I could command, having seen how far that goes towards success in the learned professions.

I engaged a servant with a handsome

livery to deliver my bills at the most respectable doors, and attend upon me when I addressed the public.

I had a thousand bills printed representing myself as Dr. Scott from Edinburgh, and I furnished myself with testimonials from respectable parties; I mean that would have been, but who in point of fact had no existence: and printed them at the foot of my bills.

My plan was on entering a town first to go for the more respectable customers by putting up at a good inn, making friends with the landlord, and sending my footman round with my bills—but before leaving I used to appear in my true colours as an itinerant quack.

In this capacity I used to harangue the people and sell my drugs.

In my public discourses I always ran down the regular practitioner, as we are all obliged to do, and the plan I used to follow was cool irony—I found this went farther than pretending to get into a heat.

Unlike most quacks I did not apply one or two remedies to every disorder, and I met with wonderful success, especially with the women : partly I think because with them imagination goes far, and my patter inspired them with more confidence than the regular doctors could, not having the gift of the gab.

While travelling as a doctor I never would accept money from any of my patients until the disease, whatever it might be, took a turn for the better ; and even then my charges were always low : but to make up I did pass a deal of base coin wherever I travelled.

The following were some of my most remarkable cures :—

The landlady of a public-house at York of a dysentery.

At Wakefield I reduced an imposthume which the proprietor was going to have cut, if it had not been for me.

At Hull I actually cured a respectable woman of a cataract, and was praised in the public journals.

These and a hundred ordinary cures are the benefits I rendered the public in return for the many wrongs I have done it.

I had been practising pharmacy some three months when one day I received a letter from Newcastle.

It was from Miss B.'s uncle telling me I might visit her now.

The letter was very short, and there was something about it I did not understand; so that, instead of filling me with delight as such a letter would a while ago, I set out for Newcastle flush of cash but full of perplexity

I reached Newcastle, and lest her friends should have changed their mind again, and receive me with an affront, I went to an alehouse convenient to her residence, and sent for her younger brother, who had never been so much against me as the others.

He came directly, and I began to put a
dozen questions to him : but he maintained
silence : he hung his head and said, ' Don't ask
me—you will soon know—and since you are
here, come without loss of time,' and he led
the way in gloomy silence.

I was taken into the house, and after some
little delay was allowed to go up into her
room—I shall never forget it.

Her cheeks that used to be like two roses
were now pale and ghastly, and her beaming
eyes were dull and sunk in her head; only
her voice and her smile were as sweet as ever.

Her first word was 'I have only waited
for this—' then she stretched out her hand
and thanked me in a sweet and composed
tone of voice ' for coming to perform the last
part of a husband's duty '—but here her feelings overcame her, and the poor thing burst
into a flood of tears, and I fell on my knees
and sobbed and cried with her, and her rela-
tions somehow felt that they were not to come

between us any more now, and they looked at one another and left the room without any noise, and we were alone a little while.

And then I kneeled down again and prayed her to forgive the injury I had done her person and character—and then she answered like a woman that she was to blame and not I—and this answer from her, and she dying, went through me like a knife, and I prayed to die for her, or at least to die with her; and bursting into unmanly and useless grief, and grovelling in anguish and remorse upon the floor, some of them came in and interfered for her sake, and very properly led me away —and not in an unkind manner, for which may God bless them any way.

I hope your reverence may never feel as I did—I had no acute sense of grief or pain— bodily or mental pain would have been a relief—I felt dead—my body seemed dead, my heart seemed dead.

I crawled to my inn, and crawled into bed,

and lay sleepless but motionless till daybreak. Then I rose and went down to the river-side and walked up and down—and at about nine, when I thought the family would be up, I went to the house.

The moment I came in sight of the house, I saw all the shutters were up. But it gave me scarcely any shock, for I was stone, and I seemed to know before this that all was over.

They wished me to see her, but I was unable then—but the day before she was buried I took a last look at her—it did not seem to be her but only some shell or frame she had once inhabited—now a ruinous heap of corruption : and that is an awful word.

Is it a castle,—there was a time when the heart of the bold soldier burned with ardour to defend it.

Is it a senate,—there was a time when the loud applause of eloquence thundered from its roof—

Or is it a temple,—there was a time when

the white-stoled priest called down the fire from heaven to bless the sacrifice.

But here is a temple, one not made with hands, the architecture of which is too sublime for our minds to conceive, a temple that was erected to be the seat of its Maker, one in which dwelt not only the image but the spirit of its Creator: let me ask then why was it thus left desolate, and whither has its tenant gone?

Tell me, ye seas, whose waves roll and ripple at our feet or thunder on our vessels, tell me have ye seen the airy stranger float along your surface, and whither has it winged its way?

Tell me, ye winds, harpers of the mountain forest; methinks ye could; for there are times ye whisper gently and seem as if ye were holding communion with departed spirits; tell me, have ye seen this airy stranger, and whither has she gone? Tell me, ye dazzling worlds that perform your regular but mystic dance upon the airy surface; tell me, have ye seen this airy stranger wing her way through your aerial canopy, and whither has it gone?

Such thoughts as these followed the first anguish at losing her, and to all these inquiries one answer seemed to come back to me from all Creation—

'The body returns to the dust, and the soul to God who gave it.'

And when I compared this answer with my own conduct, I felt I was far behind: and over my poor sweetheart's grave I vowed to amend my life—that one day I might hope to meet her again. The first three days after the funeral I tried in every direction for an honest situation.

The fourth I fell from all my good resolutions.

In my despair I had recourse to drink, and was undone. I was drunk for a whole week, and by the end of that time was penniless.

Let mankind take warning by my fate, and

not fancy the habit of drink can be formed with safety. Up to this time, though like all the world I had wasted a large portion of my gains upon drink, yet I had never gone at it like a madman. But what of that; the habit was formed, it was there waiting like a lion for its prey, waiting for a great opportunity your reverence—one came—I was in despair, —my appetite was gone, and drink comforted my stomach: my heart was dead, and drink made it beat. I had recourse to this solace, and became a beast. As I said before, for a whole week I was never not to say sober.

No man and no woman is safe that has once formed the fatal habit of looking to drink for solace—or cheerfulness—or comfort. (H.) While the world goes well they will likely be temperate : but the habit is built, the railroad to destruction is cut ready for use, the trains are laid down, and the station-houses erected; and the train is on the line waiting only for the locomotive. Well the first great trouble or hopeless grief is the locomotive : it comes to us, it grapples us, and away we go in a moment down the line we have been years constructing like a flash of lightning to the devil.

I woke one afternoon sober and penniless.

From drunkenness to thieving is not a very wide leap even to those who are beginning an evil career—to me it was no more than crossing a gutter. I pawned my watch and got on board the steamer for London, and back to my old haunts.

I soon fell in with an old pal and borrowed £10 of him and began first to pass and after that to coin ' shoffle ; ' and, when that was not quick work enough, took to house-breaking and shop-lifting again.

But in the early part of this chapter of my career, having very little cash, for part of the £10 went for clothes, I was obliged to be moderate in my expenses, and I accordingly spent a week in a lodging-house kept by an old friend of mine, which I will try to describe.

The house itself is divided into two separate compartments besides the bed-chambers.

The first or state apartment is for professional thieves.

The back room is for those street trades that lie between thieving and commerce.

My friend ushered me in here, and there were more than a score of them all gazing with their mouths open at the new comer—all engaged at various labours, and talking a dozen different branches of cant.

Some were making mats—some arranging articles for sale in their baskets or on their trays—some making matches—the 'askers' selling their begged bread at three halfpence the pound—another tuning up his fiddle—the whole lot comparing notes to the detriment of the public—the beggar telling the match-maker at what house they gave him meat or money—the hawker and mat-maker exchanging the same sort of profitable information, by which many an easy-going gentleman, that thinks himself obscure, gets his habits published among the dregs of society, and perhaps a nickname tacked on to him, and more people knowing him by it than know him by his own.

Then there was the 'buzzer' practising his necromancy—presently in came a 'sneaker' with half a firkin of butter for sale at 4d. per pound—on which the women fell to abusing their men because they had not enough money to buy ten or twelve pounds—children crying —and all in a mighty way because the fountain is not boiling.

In the corner was a handsome young female evidently a stranger, biting the end of her apron-string, her mind not being able to comprehend the fulness of the scene.

'Here is a sweetheart for you and all,' said my friend. 'She is waiting for her husband to come back,' added he winking to me.

Her husband, as she had called the man who had enticed her from her friends, never came back, and indeed nobody except herself ever thought he would.

Then to amuse her mind I requested her to go an errand for me—she agreed—I gave her a base sovereign and sent her to buy groceries, which when she had done I invited her to take tea with me, and over our tea she told me her story without reserve.

Finding she was a decent girl, and apparently had never made but this one slip, I determined to enter into partnership with her if she would consent.

Strange as it may appear I felt the want of a female companion now in a way I never had until Miss B.'s death. I believe my nerves were shaken by that sad event, and I began to want to see a woman's face opposite me, and to hear the soft notes of a female voice.

Three days after our first meeting we were

married according to the custom of the house
—i. e., a traveller dressed in a white sheet
with holes cut for his arms read a few sentences of the marriage-service to us—he then
drew a line on the floor with a piece of chalk
and made us leap over it in succession while
he recited in a solemn voice the following :

> ' Leap rogue, and follow jade,
> Man and wife for evermore.'

Which concluded the ceremony, and we
were man and wife in the eyes of all the
lodgers, unless we should agree to be untied,
which could only be done by the same party
or his successor, and with other ceremonies,
and above all—fees ! We soon left this house
and set up a lodging of our own. She made
me very comfortable when I was at home, and
I let her want for nothing.

I lived nearly three years in London this
bout, and, owing to the company I kept, I got
the cockney phrase and twang, so that I fear
I will never entirely get rid of them.

Indeed I am commonly taken for a cockney, which is a sad disgrace to a man born north of the Tweed. (I.)

At the end of this time my wife's friends sent to beg her to come home, which she asked my leave to do—I consented, and we were untied and parted with mutual expressions of esteem. Finding London rather dull after she was gone, I agreed to join a gang of us that were about to make a provincial trip.

We went to Mortimer, a village in Berkshire—the scene of our business was Reading and its neighbourhood—we committed some very daring robberies in Reading and Caversham, that will not soon be forgotten.

We broke into one house in Reading in open day—it was Sunday and the whole family were gone to church—we rifled the house and left a paper on the table, on which, I am ashamed (J.) to tell your reverence, I wrote—

'Watch as well as pray!!'

But this could not last for ever. I had been out fishing all day (a sport I am very fond of) when returning towards dusk I saw a strange face at one of the windows of our house.

Not quite understanding this, I turned back and went a mile round, to where I could see the back of the house without being recognised—and my caution was not wasted.

I soon found that the house was in the possession of the police, and that all or most of my comrades were nabbed.

Having some money about me I decamped, and returning to town found two of my companions about to start for California, dazzled by the accounts we heard of the fortunes made there by digging and levying the road-side tax on those who dug.

I joined them, and after a voyage of six months we landed at San Francisco.

Your reverence has often heard me talk of my adventures in that country, and you have often forbade me to be always thinking and talking about gold—I will therefore abstain from relating my adventures in the New World—in fact they would of themselves fill a volume—suffice it to say I had at one time twelve hundred pounds in money and gold-dust, but I wasted the greater part, and by a just retribution was robbed of the rest.

I returned to London with £10 and a nugget, which I sold for £25 in Threadneedle Street.

And now, not liking the smoke of London, after one or two successful jobs which swelled my stock to a matter of £60, I bought some new clothes, and went down to Reading, but not thinking it prudent to remain there long, I crossed the river and went into Oxford-shire.

I heard of a farmer who sometimes took a lodger, and as I was well dressed and he too honest to be suspicious, we soon came to terms.

The farmer was George Fielding, of whom your reverence has often heard me speak.

I never met with such a character as his: he did not seem to know anything about lying, far less taking anything without paying for it.

When I first lodged with him I had of course an eye to business, but I got so fond of him (K.) I could not take anything of his—and he was attached to me too, until one unlucky day he found out my real character; and then he insulted me—and now he despises me.

I spent four innocent months here, and I often thought, if I could have such a honest man as George Fielding always close to my side all day, I could keep from taking anything all the rest of my life—but unluckily my money gradually melted; in which state I went to a fair in the neighbourhood—I saw a rich farmer take out some notes and make a payment, and put the rest back into a side-pocket—almost before it reached the bottom of his pocket it was in mine.

The country banks close at three o'clock, and it was near four at the time—I got rid therefore of the Bank of England notes, meaning to change the others when a good opportunity should occur.

But meantime I suppose measures were taken against me—any way the police came down from London, and I was seized, identified, and put to an open shame.

This, the last passage of my life, went nearer to drive me to despair than all the rest; for I had begun to taste the sweets of innocence, and to love honesty under the name of George Fielding.

I was convicted at the assizes, and being recognized as having been seven times in prison, and notoriously guilty of many felonies besides, they sentenced me to twelve months' imprisonment, and transportation for ten years.

I have been six months in this gaol, where I have met with most cruel treatment, being forced to labour beyond my strength even when weakened by sickness; and punished for mere inability : and, besides the harm this wrought my body, it hardened my heart and made me look on mankind as my enemy.

But, after that, your reverence was sent here by Heaven to our relief.

It was my good fortune to find in you a gentleman whose heart was large enough to feel for all who suffer, and whose understanding could comprehend that a convict is a man, and this has been a godsend to me, and may the Almighty bless you for all your goodness, and above all for your constant battle to save us poor fellows' souls, and, when you stand one day at the great tribunal, may many a black sheep stand round you that the world perhaps took for goats to the last!

Well, sir, when I look back upon my past life, of which what I have written here is no more than a single page out of volumes and volumes, when I think of the many opportunities I have had of doing good to myself and others, and then think of how it all ends—a convicted felon, doomed to pass the remainder of my life in shame and exile, debarred from situations where I could execute my talents, and felon printed upon me, I am whiles tempted to put the gas-pipe that is in my cell into my mouth, and suck the poisonous vapour into my lungs, and thus with crime to end a life of crime. But then your face rises up before me and expostulates with a look, and bids me be patient and hope—also your words that I ought to be thankful to God for his mercy in giving me time to reflect on the enormity of my crimes, and not cutting me down as a cumberer of the ground.

But, above all, I feel it would be ungrateful to you and grieve you if I was to make away with myself under your eye ; or even to despair.

I will try my best to be somebody yet if only for your reverence's sake ; for it is a shame a gentleman like you should give his days and his nights, and all the blood in his heart, to saving us poor fellows from perdition, and be continually disappointed.

So once more thanking your reverence for all kindness, and for setting me to write this, which has amused and whiled away some weary hours, and begging you to excuse all faults and blunders, for in my busy life writing is an art I have had no time to give my mind to, I close this record of the disgraceful past, and, here in my cell, envying the cripple round whom the free air plays and on whom the sun shines, I await the gloomy future.

Thomas　*

　　—*alias* Wilkinson,

　　—*alias* Lyon,

　　—*alias* McPherson,

　　—*alias* Scott,

　　—*alias* Howard,

　　—*alias* Robinson.

A. —— 'Collected' and 'took with me.'
No such thing. 'Stole' is the word that re-
presents the transactions. Always be precise!
Never tamper with words : call a spade a spade
and a picklock a picklock—that is the first
step towards digging instead of thieving.

B. —— She did not fall on her knees—
you put that in for stage effect, and it produces none—the gesture is so manifestly in-
appropriate.

C. —— And he lent it you. Pause a moment and look at yourself by the side of this
honest, (irascible?), and magnanimous honest
man; whose hand a single paragraph of yours
made me long to grasp in mine.

D. —— 'When its topic would run to that
portion which forms the golden part of Cupid's
dart.'—This sentence is rank nonsense—no
more of this or I shall fear I have warmed a
poetaster.

E. —— 'Oh cursed night and place that robbed a virgin of her purity.' 'And oh cursed Tyne' that did not turn policeman—and oh blessed Robinson that was alone to blame. Why what bombast is this?—Always put the saddle on the right horse! and don't be so fond of cursing—believe me it is a bad habi You cursed Mr. Hawes who needed all our prayers—you cursed him in earnest: and now you are off at a tangent evading those just expressions of serious self-reproach proper to the situation, and cursing in jest the coaly Tyne, benefactor of a province, and the night a blessing wide as the world.   Bless and curse not!

F —— The turning-point of your life. Had you stayed at Newcastle and faced it out like a man, there would have been a storm, I grant you—the old chemist would have raved: but Nature is strong; for his daughter's sake he would have ended by marrying you to her, and you would be master of the shop now—an honest citizen of Newcastle—but though you had given up theft you had not forgotten how to lie.

Observe!—this is a new starting-point; all the rest of your life will be a consequence of that single falsehood—so now we shall see whether the Bible is wrong in its hatred and terror of a lie.

G. —— You did not love her—don't flatter yourself—if a thief loved a woman he would steal her; if a five-pound note had been as easy to filch from the old chemist as this poor girl, I know who would have taken it, collected it, removed it, abstracted it, and changed its relative situation. You never loved her. But I fear she loved you.

H. —— Real wisdom and observation in this remark.

I. —— Why is a twang worse than a

brogue? and why should it disgrace the native of a small nation to be taken for the native of a great nation? Is a sucker nobler than its tree??

J. —— 'Ashamed?'—the little humbug could not resist showing me his wit, of which he says he is ashamed.

K. —— That I can readily believe of you, and it is by your affections we must try and save you with God's help.

I sum up your career as Dr. Johnson did the " Beggar's Opera."
'Here is a labefaction of all principle.
   Many good impulses——dug in sand.
   Many good feelings——unstable as water.
   Many good resolves——written in air.
But not the thousandth part of a grain of principle.'

But how human your sad story is in every part; yet there are people who will dream that you and your fellows are monsters, and prescribe monstrous remedies for your souls.

I thank you for the general candour of your narrative: it renders my task a little easier.

I have many things to say to you seriously and sadly about points in this story: above all I must show you that you are not innocent of poor Miss B.'s death, whose unhappy fate has made me very sad—my poor fellow, you have not yet comprehended how much this poor girl loved you: nor the variety of tortures she was enduring all the while you were jaunting it at your ease all over the world. These killed her—I will make you see this and repent far more deeply than you have done. Half the cruelty in the world comes by want of intelligence.

I must compliment you on your literary powers—this is really an astonishing composition for a complete novice: I observe that towards the close of it, short as it is, you have already become a better writer than you were at starting—your style more disengaged, fewer Sir Ablative Absolutes, polysyllables, involved sentences, and less ungrammatical eloquence.

If it will give you any pleasure to hear it, know that in a pretty large experience of scholars, artists, lawyers, and men of business, I never encountered a man with livelier and more versatile powers than yourself. You ought to be leading the House of Commons; and you are here!

I do not however admire most the passages on which you probably pride yourself; for instance the sublime passage beginning ' Is it a castle?'

Here rhetoric intruded unseasonably upon feeling. The plain narrative of your poor sweetheart's death-bed, of her telling you woman-like that she was more to blame for being tempted than you for tempting her,

her death and your remorse, moistened my eyes as I read : but your sublime reflections dried them on the spot.

Your eloquence reminded me that you are a humbug, and never really loved this poor girl : all the worse for you.

You felt, and feel remorse, and shall feel more, but you never loved Miss B. : do not flatter yourself.

It is hardly fair to dissect the sublime ; still permit me with due timidity and respect to suggest that you have taken similitudes and called them distinctions — contrasted where you should have compared. A mouldering castle—a mute senate-house—and a ruined temple are not unlike, but like, an inanimate body.

What says the poet writing of a skull ?

' Can all that saint, sage, sophist, ever writ,
People this lonely hall, this tenement refit ? '

In matters literary begin with logic ; build on that rhetoric or what ornaments you will.

In matters moral begin with a grain of sense and principle, and on them raise the ingenuity and versatile talents of Mr. Thomas Robinson! Thus you shall not sublimely stumble in letters, nor in conduct be an ingenious, able, versatile, gifted, clever, blockhead and fool.

You called the nightingale ' him.'

This shocks an innocent prejudice.

In science, it is to be feared, there are cock nightingales. But you were favouring us with a poetic touch, and in poetry nightingales are all hens.

Remind me some day to tell you the story of Philomele.

Your closing sentences are sad, and would make me as sad or sadder if I saw your real mind in them : but this is only a temporary despondency, the effect of separate confinement, which is beginning to tell on you spite of all we can do.

I shall get your sentence shortened, and

you will soon cross the water : so you see there is nothing to despond about — your prospects were never so bright—you are now master of one craft and well advanced in others—you are at no man's mercy—your own hands avail to feed, and keep, and clothe you. Be honest and you will always be well off. Consecrate your talents to God's service and you will most likely be happy even in this world. And for the short time you have to remain in confinement we will find you all the occupation and amusement the law permits : and if you ever feel greatly depressed, ring that moment for Evans or me and we will chase the foul fiend away.

So cheer up and don't fancy you are alone, when by putting out your hand you can bring an honest fellow to your side who pities you, and me who love you.

F. E.

PRISON THOUGHTS.

Caged in a prison cell, how sad, yet true,
Does the lone heart bring former scenes to view,
Till the racked mind with bitter frensy driven,
Maligns the just decrees of Man and Heaven.
The grated barrs, and iron studded door,
The cold bare walls, and chilly pavement floor,
The hammock, table, stool, and pious book,
The jailors stealthy tread, and jealous look,
Force back the maddened thoughts to other days,
When joyous youth was crowned with hopeful bays :
E'er rank luxuriant Folly reigned supreme,
As if this Life was nothing but a dream,
Or the dire Cup had seared the unblighted heart,,
And caused all holy feelings to depart,—
E'er Each sweet hour so innocently gay,
Passed like a mellow Summers' eve away.

Cursed be the hour, when first I turned astray.

From keeping sacred Gods own hallowed day—,

When first I learned to sip the poisoned bowl,

That kills the body and corrupts the soul.

'Twas then my godly lessons, one by one,

Fled from my giddy heart till all were gone,

And left behind a waste and dreary wild,

A conscience hardened; and a soul defiled.

—Oh! when I think on what I've been; and see,

My present state, and think what I may be,

Dispair, and horror, burns and boils within,

For years of Folly and continued sin;

Untill my brain seems bursting with the dread,

Of Heaven's just judgments falling on my head.

No banefull passions fired my tranquill mind,

No wild unruly thoughts ranged unconfined,

But all was fair, and gladsome as the grove,

Where warbling songsters live in artless love—.

—How changed my lot,—No Sister, Mother, Sire,

Now fondly sit, around the wintry fire;

No household song beguiles the lengthened night,

No homely jest creates a fond delight,

No sabbath morning sees us now engage,

In rap't attention on the holy page,

Or hears the swelling notes of praise and prayer,

Borne on the breese, & floating on the Air.

Oh! could my parents shades but bend on earth,
They'd mourn like me the morning of my birth. .
—Almighty Father!—God of Life and Death, !
Give, oh! give *me*, a true and living Faith,
Bestow Thy quickening Spirit, and impart
Thy saving Grace to tranquillise my heart,
That I may better live, for time to come,
And rear my spirit for Thy heavenly home,!.

THE LAW AND THE GOSPEL.

A Sermon preached in the Chapel of   *   Jail, on Sunday,
9th January, 1849, from Matthew 5th and 17th, by the Rev.
Francis Eden and versified

BY ONE OF THE PRISONERS.

'Mid rolling clouds of fearfull smoke,
　'Mid lightnings flash, and thunders roar,
'Mid loud continued sounds, which shook,
　The startled earth from shore to shore, !
'Mid volumes of devouring flame,
Unseen, yet felt, the Almighty came, !

Lo ! on Mount Sinia's giddy height,
　Is reared Jehovahs awfull throne,
Pregnant with Heavens ethereal light,
　Too glorious to be gazed upon,
While beams of dazzling brightness bound
Tho Circuit of the hallowod ground ;

Hark ! as the Appalling voice of God,
   Proclaims the Law of Life and Death,
Nature, o'erburdened with the load,
   Holds hard her almost fleeting breath.
While sunless heaven, and darkned air
—Are hung with blackness of dispair, !

Offspring of Gentile, and of Jew,
   Descendants of a common stock,
These great eternal Laws for you
   Were thundered from Mount Sinia's rock ;
And ill or good on him shall fall,
Who breaks but one, or keeps them all.

But oh ! weak man can n'eer obey,
   Laws with such fearfull justice fraught.
For every moment of the day
   He sins in Word or deed, or thought.
The Law of Death would thus enslave him,
Did not a pardoning Gospel save him,,

From Calvary's hill a stream proceeds,
   Whose cleansing merits all may share,
Aye, even although their guilt exceeds
   The weight of what the earth can bear.
For Christs atoning blood can clean,
A hell deserving world from sin.

No lightnings flash, no scowling sky,
  No trembling mount of smoke and flamc,
No crashing thunder boomed from high,
  When our Great Mediator came:
But Seraphs sounds announced to earth
Glad tidings of a Saviours birth.

No chosen consecrated priest,
  No hcaps of slain or seas of blood,
Nor solemn Fast, nor stated Feast,
  Can now appease a Jealous God,
Or open up a Fount of Grace,
To Adams unregenerate race,

An humble heart, a lowly mind,
  A contrite and believing soul,
Where Truth and Mercy are enshrined,
  Beyond a sinfull world's controul,
Is all the God of Heaven will claim,
From those who own Immanuels name; !

How goodly are the steps of those,
  Who walk in humbleness of heart,
And with well grounded hopes have chose
  The Gospels sure and better part.
To such the Law of works is dead,
Through Faith in Christ, thoir living head.

But, as Jehovahs dread decree,
   Does with a Saviours Love unite,
So let our Faith and Works agree,
   In one continued bond of Light:
For Faith, and Works, if used alone,
Can n'eer for guilty deeds atone.

Then fly ye Sinners to the Cross,
   There let your eager hopes be bound,
Count all things else but dung and dross,
   To win Christ, and in him be found,
So shall your Christian race be blest,
With Heavens prepared Eternal Rest!

                    *   *Jail*, *3rd Feby* 1848.

Prisoner's name—THOMAS ROBINSON.

JACK OF ALL TRADES.

A Matter-of-Fact Romance.

JACK OF ALL TRADES.

A Matter-of-Fact Romance.

THERE are nobs in the world, and there are snobs.

I regret to say I belong to the latter department.

There are men that roll through life, like a fire new red ball going across Mr. Lord's cricket-ground on a sunshiny day; there is another sort that have to rough it in general, and above all to fight tooth and nail for the quartern-loaf—and not always win the battle; I am one of this lot.

One comfort, folk are beginning to take an

F 2

interest in us; I see nobs of the first water looking with a fatherly eye into our affairs, our leaden taxes and feather incomes, our fifteen per cent. on undeniable security when the rich pay but three and a half; our privations and vexations; our dirt and distresses; and one day a literary gent, that knows my horrible story, assured me that my ups and downs would entertain the nobility gentry and commonalty of these realms.

'Instead of grumbling to me,' says he 'print your troubles: and I promise you all the world will read them, and laugh at them.'

'No doubt sir,' said I rather ironical, 'all the world is at leisure for that.'

'Why look at the signs of the times,' says he, 'can't you see workmen are up? so take us while we are in the humour and that is now. We shall not always be for squeezing honey out of weeds, shall we?' 'Not likely sir,' says I. Says he 'how nice it will be to growl wholesale to a hundred thousand of

your countrymen (which they do love a bit
of a growl) instead of growling retail to a
small family that has got hardened to you!'
And there he had me; for I am an Englishman, and proud of it, and attached to all the
national habits, except delirium tremens. In
short, what with him inflaming my dormant
conceit, and me thinking 'well I can but say
my say and then relapse into befitting silence,'
I did one day lay down the gauge and take
up the pen, in spite of my wife's sorrowful
looks.

She says nothing, but you may see she
does not believe in the new tool, and that is
cheerful and inspiriting to a beginner.

However there is a something that gives me
more confidence than all my literary friend
says about ' workmen being up in the literary
world' and that is that I am not the hero of
my own story.

Small as I sit here behind my wife's
crockery, and my own fiddles, in this thunder-

ing hole, Wardour Street, I was for many
years connected with one of the most cele-
brated females of modern times; her adventures run side by side with mine; she is the
bit of romance that colours my humble life,
and my safest excuse for intruding on the
public.

CHAPTER I.

FATHER and mother lived in King Street Soho: he was a fiddle-maker, and taught me the A B C of that science—at odd times; for I had a regular education, and a very good one at a school in West Street. This part of my life was as smooth as glass; my troubles did not begin till I was thirteen: at that age my mother died, and then I found out what she *had been* to me: that was the first and the worst grief; the next I thought bad enough; coming in from school one day about nine months after her death, I found a woman sitting by the fire opposite father.

I came to a stand in the middle of the floor, with two eyes like saucers staring at the pair so my father introduced me.

'This is your new mother! Anne this is John!'

'Come and kiss me John,' says the lady. Instead of which John stood stock still, and burst out roaring and crying without the. least leaving off staring, which to be sure was a cheerful encouraging reception for a lady just come into the family. I roared pretty hard for about ten seconds, then stopped dead short, and says I, with a sudden calm, the more awful for the storm that had raged before, 'I'll go and tell Mr. Paley!' and out I marched.

Mr. Paley was a little hump-backed tailor with the heart of a dove and the spirit of a lion or two. I made his acquaintance through pitching into two boys, that were queering his protuberances all down Princes Street, Soho; a kind of low humour he detested:

and he had taken quite a fancy to me : we were hand and glove the old man and me.

I ran to Paley and told him what had befallen upon the house ; he was not struck all of a heap as I thought he would be ; and he showed me it was legal, of which I had not an idea, and his advice was 'put a good face on it, or the house will soon be too hot to hold you boy'

He was right : I don't know whether it was my fault or hers, or both's, but we could never mix. I had seen another face by that fireside and heard another voice in the house that seemed to me a deal more melodious than hers, and the house did become hotter, and the inmates' looks colder, than agreeable ; so one day I asked my father to settle me in some other house not less than a mile from King Street Soho. He and step-mother jumped at the offer, and apprenticed me to Mr. Dawes. Here I learned more mysteries of guitar-making, violin-making, etc. etc. ;

and lived in tolerable comfort nearly four years; there was a ripple on the water though. My master had a brother, a thickset heavy fellow, that used to bully my master, especially when he was groggy, and less able to take his own part. My master being a good fellow I used to side with him, and this brought me a skinful of sore bones more than once, I can tell you. But one night after some months of peace, I heard a terrible scrimmage, and running down into the shop-parlour I found Dawes junior pegging into Dawes senior no allowance, and him crying blue murder.

I was now an able-bodied youth between sixteen and seventeen years of age, and, having a little score of my own with the attacking party, I opened quite silent and business-like with a one, two, and knocked him into a corner flat perpendicular: he was dumbfounded for a moment, but the next he came out like a bull at me. I stepped on one side and met him

with a blow on the side of the temple and
knocked him flat horizontal; and when he
offered to rise I shook my fist at him and
threatened him he should come to grief if he
dared to move.

At this he went on quite a different lay:
he lay still and feigned dissolution with con-
siderable skill, to frighten us; and I can't say
I felt easy at all, but my master, who took
cheerful views of everything in his cups, got
the enemy's tumbler of brandy and water, and,
with hiccups and absurd smiles and a teaspoon,
deposited the contents gradually on the various
parts of his body.

' Lez revive 'm ! ' said he.

This was low life to come to pass in a
repectable tradesman's back-parlour.   But
when grog comes in at the door good
manners walk to the window, ready to take
leave if requested.   Where there is drink
there is always degradation of some sort or
degree; put that in your tumblers and sip it !

After this no more battles. The lowly apprentice's humble efforts (pugilistic) restored peace to his master's family.

Six months of calm industry now rolled over, and then I got into trouble by my own fault.

Looking back upon the various fancies, and opinions, and crotchets, that have passed through my head at one time or another, I find that, between the years of seventeen and twenty-four, a strange notion beset me; it was this; that women are all angels.

For this chimera I now began to suffer, and continued to at intervals till the error was rooted out—with their assistance.

There were two women in my master's house, his sister, aged twenty-four, and his cook aged thirty-seven; with both these I fell ardently in love; and so, with my sentiments, I should have with six, had the house held half a dozen. Unluckily my affections were not accompanied with the discretion so ticklish a situation called for. The ladies found one another out, and I fell a victim to the virtuous indignation that fired three bosoms.

The cook, in virtuous indignation that an apprentice should woo his master's sister, told my master.

The young lady, in virtuous indig. that a boy should make a fool of 'that old woman,' told my master, who, unluckily for me, was now the quondam Dawes junior; Dawes senior having retired from the active business and turned sleeping and drinking partner

My master whose v. i. was the strongest of the three, since it was him I had leathered, took me to Bow Street, made his complaint, and forced me to cancel my indentures; the cook with tears packed up my Sunday suit, the young lady opened her bedroom door three inches and shut it with a don't-come-anigh-me slam; and I drifted out to London with eighteen-pence and my tools.

On looking back on this incident of my life,

I have a regret; a poignant one; it is that some good Christian did not give me a devilish good hiding into the bargain then and there.

I did not feel quite strong enough in the spirits to go where I was sure to be blown up; so I skirted King Street and entered the Seven Dials, and went to Mr. Paley and confessed my sins.

How differently the same thing is seen by different eyes! all the morning I had been called a young villain, first by one then by another, till at last I began to see it: Mr. Paley viewed me in the light of martyr, and I remember I fell into his views on the spot.

Paley was a man that had his little theory about women and it differed from my juvenile one.

He held that women are at bottom the seducers, men the seduced. 'The men court the women I grant you, but so it is the fish that runs after the bait,' said he. 'The

women draw back? yes, and so does the
angler draw back the bait when the fish are
shy, don't he? and then the silly gudgeons
misunderstand the move, and make a rush at
it, and get hooked—like you.'

Holding such vile sentiments he shifted all
the blame off my shoulders; he turned to and
abused the whole gang, as he called the family
in Litchfield Street I had just left, instead of
reading me the lesson for the day, which he
ought, and I should have listened to from him
—perhaps.

'Now then, don't hang your head like
that,' shouted the spunkey little fellow,
'snivelling and whimpering at your time of
life! we are going to have a jolly good
supper, you and I, that is what *we* are going
to do; and you shall sleep here: my daughter
is at school, you shall have her room. I am
in good work—thirty shillings a week—that
is plenty for three, Lucy and you and me,'
(himself last). 'Your father isn't worth a

bone button, and your mother isn't worth the shank to it : I'm your father, and your mother into the bargain, for want of a better : you live with me and snap your fingers at Dawes and all his crew—ha ha—a fine loss to be sure—the boy is a fool—cooks and coquettes and fiddle-touters, rubbish not worth picking up out of a gutter—they be d——d.'

And so I was installed in Miss Paley's apartment, Seven Dials; and nothing would have made my adopted parent happier than for me to be put my hands in my pockets, and live upon goose and cabbage. But downright laziness was never my character. I went round to all the fiddle-shops and offered, as bold as brass, to make a violin, a tenor, or a bass, and bring it home. Most of them looked shy at me, for it was necessary to trust me with the wood, and to lend me one or two of the higher class of tools, such as a turning-saw, and a jointing-plane.

At last I came to Mr. Dodd in Berners

Street; here my father's name stood me in stead. Mr. Dodd risked his wood and the needful tools, and in eight days I brought him with conceit and trepidation mixed in equal part, a violin, which I had sometimes feared it would frighten him, and sometimes hoped it would charm him. He took it up, gave it one twirl round, satisfied himself it was a fiddle, good bad or indifferent, put it in the window along with the rest, and paid for it as he would for a penny roll. I timidly proposed to make another for him; he grunted a consent, which it did not seem to me a rapturous one.

Mr. Metzler also ventured to give me work of this kind. For some months I wrought hard all day, and amused myself with my companions all the evening, selecting my pals from the following classes: small actors, showmen, pedestrians, and clever discontented mechanics; one lot I never would have at any price, and that was the stupid ones, that could only booze and could not tell me anything I did not know about pleasure, business, and life.

This was a bright existence : so it came to a full stop.

At one and the same time Miss Paley came home, and the fiddle-trade took one of those chills all fancy trades are subject to.

No work—no lodging without paying for it —no wherewithal.

CHAPTER II.

JOHN BEARD, a friend of mine, was a painter and grainer. His art was to imitate oak, maple, walnut, satin-wood, etc., etc., upon vulgar deal, beech, or what not.

This business works thus: first a coat of oil-colour is put on with a brush, and this colour imitates what may be called the background of the wood that is aimed at: on this oil-background the champ, the fibre, the grain and figure, and all the incidents of the superior wood, are imitated by various manœuvres in water-colours; or rather in beer-colours, for beer is the approved medium. A coat of varnish over all gives a look of unity to the work.

Beard was out of employ; so was I; bitter against London; so was I. He sounded me about trying the country, and I agreed; and this was the first step of my many travels.

We started the next day; he with his brushes and a few colours and one or two thin panels painted by way of advertisement; and I with hope, inexperience, and three-pence. On the road we spent this and his five-pence, and entered the town of Brentford towards nightfall as empty as drums, and as hungry as wolves.

What was to be done? After a long discussion we agreed to go to the mayor of the town and tell him our case, and offer to paint his street-door in the morning, if he would save our lives for the night.

We went to the mayor; luckily for us, he had risen from nothing as we were going to do ; and so he knew exactly what we meant when we looked up in his face and laid our hands on our sausage-grinders. He gave us eighteen-pence and an order on a lodging-house, and put bounds to our gratitude by making us promise to let his street-door alone ; we thanked him from our hearts, supped and went to bed, and agreed the country, (as we two cockneys called Brentford) was chock full of good fellows.

The next day up early in the morning, and away to Hounslow ; here Beard sought work all through the town : and just when we were in despair he got one door. We dined and slept on this door, but we could not sup off it : we had two-pence over though for the morning, and walked on a penny roll each to Maidenhead.

Here, as we entered the town, we passed a little house with the door painted oak, and a brass-plate announcing a plumber and glazier, and house-painter. Beard pulled up before this door in sorrowful contempt. 'Now look here, John,' says he, 'here is a fellow living among the woods, and you would swear he never saw an oak-plank in his life to look at his work.'

Before so very long we came to another specimen : this was maple, and farther from Nature than a lawyer from heaven, as the saying is. 'There, that will do,' says Beard. 'I'll tell you what it is, we must try a different move ; it is no use looking for work ; folks will only employ their own tradesmen ; we must teach the professors of the art at so much a panel.'

'Will they stomach that ?' said I.

'I think they will, as we are strangers and from London. You go and see whether there is a fiddle to be doctored in the town, and meet me again in the market-place at twelve o'clock.'

I did meet him and forlorn enough I was ; my trade had broke down in Maidenhead ; not a job of any sort.

'Come to the public-house!' was his first word: that sounded well I thought.

We sat down to bread and cheese and beer, and he told his tale.

It seems he went into a shop, told the master he was a painter and grainer from a great establishment in London, and was in the habit of travelling and instructing provincial artists in the business. The man was a pompous sort of a customer, and told Beard he knew the business as well as he did, better belike.

Beard answered—'Then you are the only one here that does; for I've been all through the town, and anything wider from the mark than their oak and maple I never saw.' Then he quietly took down his panels and spread them out, and looking out sharp he noticed a sudden change come over the man's face.

'Well' says the man, 'we reckon ourselves pretty good at it in this town. However I shouldn't mind seeing how you London chaps do it—what do you charge for a specimen?'

' My charge is two shillings a panel. What wood should you like to gain a notion of? said Beard, as dry as a chip.

' Well—satin-wood.'

Beard painted a panel of satin-wood before his eyes; and of course it was done with great ease, and on a better system than had reached Maidenhead up to that time. 'Now' says Beard 'I must go to dinner.'

' Well, come back again my lad,' says the man, ' and we will go in for something else.' So Beard took his two shillings and met me as aforesaid.

After dinner he asked for a private room. ' A private room,' said I, ' hadn't you better order our horse and gig out and go and call on the rector ? '

' None of your chaff,' says he.

When we got into the room he opened the business.

' Your trade is no good—you must take to mine.'

' What, teach painters how to paint, when I don't know a stroke myself! '

' Why not? You've only got it to learn: they have got to unlearn all they know; that is the only long process about it. I'll teach you in five minutes,' says he—' look here.' He then imitated oak before me, and made me do it. He corrected my first attempt: the second satisfied him: we then went on to maple and so through all the woods he could mimic. He then returned to his customer, and I hunted in another part of the town; and before nightfall I actually gave three lessons to two professors: it is amazing but true, that I, who had been learning ten minutes, taught men who had been all their lives at it—in the country.

One was so pleased with his tutor, that he gave me a pint of beer besides my fee. I thought he was poking fun when he first offered it me.

Beard and I met again triumphant: we

had a rousing supper and a good bed and the next day started for Henley, where we both did a small stroke of business : and on to Reading for the night.

Our goal was Bristol. Beard had friends there. But as we zig-zagged for the sake of the towns, we were three weeks walking to that city; but we reached it at last, having disseminated the science of graining in many cities, and got good clothes and money in return.

At Bristol we parted. He found regular employment the first day, and I visited the fiddle-shops and offered my services. At most I was refused; at one or two I got trifling jobs ; but at last I went to the right one. The master agreed with me for piece work on a large scale, and the terms were such that by working quick and very steady, I could make about twenty-five shillings a week. At this I kept two years, and might have longer, no doubt—but my employer's niece came to live with him.

She was a woman : and my theory being in full career at this date, mutual ardour followed, and I asked her hand of her uncle, and instead of that he gave me what the Turkish ladies get for the same offence—the sack. Off to London again, and the money I had saved by my industry just landed me in the Seven Dials and six-pence over.

I went to Paley, crestfallen as usual. He heard my story, complimented me on my energy industry and talent, regretted the existence of woman, and inveighed against her character and results.

We went that evening to private theatricals in Berwick Street, and there I fell in with an acquaintance in the firework line ; on hearing my case, he told me I had just fallen from the skies in time, his employer wanted a fresh hand.

The very next day behold me grinding and sifting and ramming powder at Somers Town, and at it ten months.

My evenings, when I was not undoing my

own work to show its brilliancy, were often spent in private theatricals.

I hear a row made just now about a dramatic school. 'We have no dramatic schools,' is the cry. Well in the day I speak of there were several; why I belonged to two. We never brought to light an actor; but we succeeded so far as to ruin more than one lad who had brains enough to make a tradesman, till we heated those brains and they boiled all away.

The way we destroyed youth was this: of course nobody would pay a shilling at the door to see us running wild among Shakspere's lines like pigs broken into a garden: so the expenses fell upon the actors; and they paid according to the value of the part each played. Richard the Third cost a puppy two pounds; Richmond fifteen shillings; and so on; so that with us, as in the big world, dignity went by wealth, not merit. I remember this made me sore at the time; still there are two sides to everything: they say poverty urges men to crime; mine saved me from it. If I could have afforded, I would have murdered one or two characters that have lived with good reputation from Queen Bess to Queen Victoria; but as I couldn't afford it, others that could did it for me.

Well, in return for his cash, Richard or Hamlet or Othello commanded tickets in proportion; for the tickets were only gratuitous to the spectators.

Consequently at night each important actor played not only to a most merciful audience, but a large band of devoted friendly spirits in it, who came not to judge him, but express to carry him through triumphant — like an election. Now, when a vain ignorant chap hears a lot of hands clapping, he has not the sense to say to himself 'paid for!' No, it is applause, and applause stamps his own secret opinion of himself: he was off his balance before, and now he tumbles heel over tip into the notion that he is a genius; throws his commercial prospects after the two pounds that went in Richard or Beverley, and crosses Waterloo Bridge spouting,

> ' A fico for the shop and poplins base !
> Counter, avaunt! I on his southern bank
> Will fire the Thames.'

Noodle thus singing goes over the water. But they won't have him at the Surrey or the Vic. : so he takes to the country : and, while his money lasts, and he can pay the mismanager of a small theatre, he gets leave to play with Richard and Hamlet. But when the money is gone and he wants to be paid for Richard & co. they laugh at him, and put him in his right place, and that is a utility, and perhaps ends a ' super. ; ' when, if he had not been a coxcomb, he might have sold ribbon like a man to his dying day.

We, and our dramatic schools, ruined more than one or two of this sort by means of his vanity in my young days.

My poverty saved me. The conceit was here in vast abundance, but not the funds to intoxicate myself with such choice liquors as Hamlet & co. Nothing above old Gobbo (five shillings) ever fell to my lot and by my talent.

When I had made and let off fireworks for a few months, I thought I could make more as a rocket-master, than a rocket-man. I had saved a pound or two. Most of my friends dissuaded me from the attempt; but Paley said, 'let him alone now—don't keep him down—he is born to rise. I'll risk a pound on him.' So, by dint of several small loans, I got the materials and made a set of fireworks myself, and agreed with the keeper of some tea-gardens at Hampstead for the spot.

At the appointed time, attended by a trusty band of friends, I put them up; and, when I had taken a tolerable sum at the door, 1 let them all off.

But they did not all profit by the permission. Some went, but others whose supposed destination was the sky, soared about as high as a house, then returned and forgot their wild nature, and performed the office of our household fires upon the clothes of my visitors; and some faithful spirits, like old domestics, would not leave their master at any price: would not take their discharge. Then there was a row, and I should have been mauled, but my guards rallied round me and brought me off with whole bones, and marched back to London with me, quizzing me and drinking at my expense. The publican refused to give me my promised fee, and my loss by ambition was twenty-eight shillings, and my reputation —if you could call that a loss.

Was not I quizzed up and down the Seven Dials! Paley alone contrived to stand out in my favour. 'Nonsense, a first attempt,' said he, 'they mostly fail: don't you give in for those fools! I'll tell you a story. There was a chap in prison—I forget his name: he lived in the old times a few hundred years ago, I can't justly say how many: he had failed—at something or other—I don't know how many times—and there he was. Well Jack, one day he notices a spider climbing up a thundering great slippery stone in the wall. She got a little way—then down she fell—up again and tries it on again—down again. Ah, says the man, you will never do it. But the spider was game—she got six falls, but, by George, the seventh trial she got up. So the gentleman says " a man ought to have as much heart as a spider: I won't give in till the seventh trial." Bless you, long before the seventh he carried all before him, and got to be king of England—or something.'

'King of England!' said I, ' that was a move upwards out of the stone jug.'

'Well,' said Paley the hopeful, ' you can't be king of England; but you may be the fire-king, he! he! if you are true to powder. How much money do you want to try again ?'

I was nettled at my failure, and fired by

Paley and his spider, I scraped together a few pounds once more, and advertised a display of fireworks for a certain Monday night.

On the Sunday afternoon Paley and I happened to walk on the Hampstead Road, and near the Adam and Eve we fell in with an announcement of fireworks. On the bill appeared in enormous letters the following.

'No connexion with the disgraceful exhibition that took place last friday week !! '

Paley was in a towering passion. 'Look here John,' says he, 'but never you mind—it won't be here long, for I'll tear it down in about half a moment.'

'No, you must not do that,' said I, a little nervous.

'Why not, you poor-spirited muff,' shouts the little fellow—'let me alone—let me get at it—what are you holding me for ?'

'No! no! no! well then—'

'Well then what ?'

' Well then it is mine.'

' What is yours ?'

' That advertisement.'

' How can it be yours when it insults you ?"

' Oh! business before vanity.'

' Well I am blest! Here's a go—look here now,' and he began to split his sides laughing; but all of a sudden he turned awful grave, ' you will rise my lad: this is genuine talent: they might as well try to keep a balloon down.' In short, my friend, who was as honest as the day in his own sayings and doings, admired this bit of rascality in me and augured the happiest results.

That district of London which is called the Seven Dials, was now divided into two great parties ; one augured for me a brilliant success next day: the other a dead failure. The latter party numbered many names unknown to fame : the former consisted of Paley. I was neuter, distrusting, not my merits, but what I called my luck.

On Monday afternoon I was busy putting out the fireworks, nailing them to their posts &c. Towards evening it began to rain so heavily that they had to be taken in, and the whole thing given up: it was postponed to Thursday

On Thursday night we had a good assembly: the sum taken at the doors exceeded my expectation. I had my misgivings on account of the rain that had fallen on my kickshaws Monday evening, so I began with those articles I had taken in first out of the rain; they went off splendidly and my personal friends were astounded; but soon my poverty began to tell: instead of having many hands to save the fireworks from wet, I had been alone, and of course much time had been lost in getting them under cover: we began now to get along the damp lot, and science was lost in chance: some would and some wouldn't, and the people began to goose me.

A rocket or two that fizzed themselves out

without rising a foot inflamed their angry passions; so I announced two fiery pigeons.

The fiery pigeon is a pretty firework enough : it is of the nature of a rocket, but being on a string it travels backwards and forwards between two termini, to which the string is fixed : when there are two strings and two pigeons, the fiery wings race one another across the ground, and charm the gazing throng. One of my termini was a tree at the extremity of the gardens ; up this tree I mounted in my shirt-sleeves with my birds : the people surrounded the tree and were dead silent : I could see their final verdict and my fate hung on these pigeons ; I placed them and with a beating heart lighted their matches. To my horror one did not move. I might as well have tried to explode green sticks. The other started and went off with great resolution and accompanying cheers towards the opposite side. But midway it suddenly stopped and the cheers with it : it did not

come to an end all at once ; but the fire oozed
gradually out of it like water—a howl of
derision was hurled up into the tree at me :
but, worse than that, looking down I saw in
the moonlight a hundred stern faces with
eyes like red-hot emeralds, in which I read
my fate : they were waiting for me to come
down, like terriers for a rat in a trap, and I
felt by the look of them that they would kill
me or near it ; I crept along a bough the end
of which cleared the wall and overhung the
road : I determined to break my neck sooner
than fall into the hands of an insulted public.
An impatient orange whizzed by my ear, and
an apple knocked my hat out of the premises,
I crouched and clung—luckily I was on an
ash-bough, long, tapering and tough ; it bent
with me like a rainbow. A stick or two now
whizzed past my ear, and it began to hail
fruit. I held on like grim death till the road
was within six feet of me, and then dropped
and ran off home, like a dog with a kettle at

his tail; meantime a rush was made to the gate to cut me off; but it was too late: the garden meandered, and my executioners, when they got to the outside, saw nothing but a flitting spectre : me in my shirt-sleeves making for the Seven Dials.

Mr. and Miss Paley were seated by their fire, and, as I afterwards learned, Paley was recommending her to me for a husband, and explaining to her at some length, why I was sure to rise in the world, when a figure in shirt-sleeves begrimed with gunpowder and no hat burst into the room, and shrank without a word into the corner by the fire.

Miss Paley looked up, and then began to look down and snigger. Her father stared at me, and after a while I could see him set his teeth and nerve his obstinate old heart for the coming struggle.

'Well, how did it happen?' said he, at last. 'Where is your coat?'

I told him the whole story.

Miss Paley had her hand to her mouth all the time, afraid to give vent to the feelings proper to the occasion because of her father.

'Now answer me one question. Have you got their money?' says Paley.

'Yes I have got their money for that matter.'

'Well then what need you care? You are all right; and if they had gone off they would have been all over by now just the same: he wants his supper Lucy—give us something hot to make us forget our squibs and crackers, or we shall die of a broken heart all us poor fainting souls—such a calamity! The rain wetted them through—that is all— you couldn't fight against the elements, could you? Lay the cloth, girl.'

'But Mr. Paley,' whined I, 'they have got my new coat; and you may be sure they have torn it limb from jacket.'

'Have they?' cried he, 'well, that is a comfort any way. Your new coat eh? Lucy,

it hung on the boy's back like an old sack.
Do you see this bit of cloth? I shall make
you a Sunday coat with this, and then you'll
sell. Fetch a quart to-night girl instead of
a pint: the fire-king is going to do us the
honour. Che-er up!!'

CHAPTER III.

It was now time that Miss Paley should
suffer the penalty of her sex. She was a
comely good-humoured and sensible girl.
We used often to walk out together on
Sundays, and very friendly we were. I used
to tell her she was the flower of her sex, and
she used to laugh at that. One Sunday I
spoke more plainly, and laid my heart, my
thirteen shillings, the fruit of my last impos-
ture on the public, and my various arts, at her
feet, out walking.

A proposal of this sort, if I may trust the
stories I read, produces thrilling effects; if

agreeable, the ladies either refuse in order to torment themselves, which act of virtue justifies them, they think, in tormenting the man they love, or else they show their rapturous assent by bursting out crying or by fainting away, or their lips turning cold, and other signs proper to a disordered stomach; if it is to be 'no' they are almost as much cut up about it, and say no like yes, which has the happy result of leaving him hope and prolonging his pain. Miss Paley did quite different. She blushed a little and smiled archly and said 'Now John you and I are good friends, and I like you very much; and I will walk with you and laugh with you as much as you like; but I have been engaged these two years to Charles Hook, and I love him, John.'

'Do you, Lucy?'

'Yes,' under her breath a bit.

'Oh!'

'So if we are to be friends you must not

put that question to me again John. What
do you say? we are to be friends, are we
not?' and she put out her hand.

'Yes, Lucy.'

'And John, you need not go for to tell my
father: what is the use vexing him? He has
got a notion ; but it will pass away in time.'

I consented of course, and Lucy and I were
friends.

Mr. Paley somehow suspected which way
his daughter's heart turned, and not long
after a neighbour told me he heard him
quizzing her unmerciful for her bad judgment. As for harshness or tyranny that was
not under his skin as the saying is. He
wound up with telling her that John was a
man safe to rise.

'I hope he may, father, I am sure,' says
Lucy.

'Well, and can't you see he is the man for
you?'

'No, father, I can't see that, he he.'

CHAPTER IV.

I DON'T think I have been penniless not a
dozen times in my life. When I get down to
twopence or threepence, which is very fre-
quent indeed, something is apt to turn up
and raise me to silver once more, and there I
stick. But about this time I lay out of work
a long time and was reduced to the lowest
ebb. In this condition a friend of mine took
me to the 'Harp' in Little Russell Street to
meet Mr. Webb the manager of a strolling
company. Mr. Webb was beating London
for recruits to complete his company which
ay at Bishops Stortford, but which owing

to desertions was not numerous enough to massacre five-act plays. I instantly offered to go as carpenter and scene-shifter: to this he demurred—he was provided with them already—he wanted actors, to this I objected, not that I cared to what sort of work I turned my hand, but in these companies a carpenter is paid for his day's work according to his agreement, but the actors are remunerated by a share in the night's profits, and the profits are often written in the following figures £0. 0s. 0d.

However Mr. Webb was firm, he had no carpenter's place to offer me, so I was obliged to lower my pretensions. I agreed then to be an actor. I was cast as Father Philip in the " Iron Chest " next evening. My share of the profits to be one-eighth. I borrowed a shilling, and my friend Johnstone and I walked all the way to Bishops Stortford. We played the " Iron Chest " and divided the profits. Hitherto I had been in the mechanical arts. This was my first step into the fine ones. Father Philip's share of the " Chest" was $2\frac{1}{2}d$.

Now this might be a just remuneration for the performance; I almost think it was : but it left the walk, thirty miles, not accounted for.

The next night I was cast in " Jerry Sneak." I had no objection to the part; only, under existing circumstances, the place to play it seemed to me to be the road to London, not the boards of Bishops Stortford; so I sneaked off towards the Seven Dials. Johnstone, though cast for the hero, was of Jerry's mind and sneaked away along with him.

We had made but twelve miles when the manager and a constable came up with us. Those were peremptory days; they offered us our choice of the fine arts again, or prison. After a natural hesitation we chose the arts, and were driven back to them like sheep. Night's profits $5d$. In the morning the whole company dissolved away like a snowball. Johnstone and I had a meagre breakfast and walked on it twenty-six miles. He was a stout fellow—shone in brigands—he encouraged and helped me along; but at last I could go no further.

My slighter frame was quite worn out with hunger and fatigue. 'Leave me,' I said, 'perhaps some charitable hand will aid me, and if not why then I shall die: and I don't care if I do; for I have lost all hope.'

'Nonsense,' cried the fine fellow. 'I'll carry you home on my back sooner than leave you—die? that is a word a man should never say   Come, courage, only four miles more.'

No. I could not move from the spot. I was what I believe seldom really happens to any man, dead beat, body and soul.

I sank down on a heap of stones. Johnstone sat down beside me.

The sun was just setting. It was a bad look out. Starving people to lie out on

stones all night. A man can stand cold and
he can fight with hunger: but put those two
together and life is soon exhausted.

At last a rumble was heard, and presently
an empty coal-waggon came up. A coal-
heaver sat on the shaft and another walked
by the side. Johnstone went to meet them—
they stopped—I saw him pointing to me, and
talking earnestly.

The men came up to me: they took hold
of me and shot me into the cart like a hundred weight of coal. 'Why he is starving
with cold,' said one of them, and he flung
half a dozen empty sacks over me, and on
we went. At the first public the waggon
stopped and soon one of my new friends
with a cheerful voice brought a pewter flagon
of porter to me: I sipped it. 'Don't be
afraid of it,' cried he, 'down with it; it is
meat and drink that is.' And indeed so I
found it. It was a heavenly solid liquid to me:
it was 'stout' by name, and 'stout' by nature.

I

These good fellows, whom men do right to call black diamonds, carried me safe into the Strand, and thence being now quite my own man again, I reached the Seven Dials. Paley was in bed. He came down directly in his night-gown, and lighted a fire and pulled a piece of cold beef out of the cupboard and cheered me as usual, but in a fatherly way this time; and of course at my age I was soon all right again, and going to take the world by storm to-morrow morning. He left me for awhile and went upstairs: presently he came down again.

'Your bed is ready, John.'

'Why,' said I, 'you have not three rooms.'

'Lucy is on a visit,' said he, then he paused. 'Stop a bit, I'll warm your bed.'

He took me upstairs to my old room and warmed the bed. I like a thoughtless young fool rolled into it, half-gone with sleep, and never woke till ten next morning.

I don't know what the reader will think of

me when I tell him that the old man had
turned Lucy out of her room into his own and
sat all night by the fire that I might lie soft
after my troubles.   Ah—he was a bit of steel.
And have you left me, and can I share no more
sorrow or joy with you in this world!   Eh
dear, it makes me misty to think of the old
man—after all these years.

CHAPTER V.

—◆—

I USED often to repair and doctor a violin for
a gent whom I shall call Chaplin: he played
in the orchestra of the Adelphi Theatre.
Mr. Chaplin was not only a customer but a
friend; he saw how badly off I was, and
had a great desire to serve me: now it so
happened that Mr. Yates the manager was
going to give an entertainment he called his
' At Homes,' and this took but a small orchestra,
of which Mr. Chaplin was to be the leader:
so he was allowed to engage the other instru-
ments; and he actually proposed to me to be
a second violin.

I stared at him. 'How can I do that?'

'Why I often hear you try a violin.'

'Yes, and I always play the same notes, perhaps you have observed that too?'

'I notice it is always a slow movement—eh? never mind, this is the only thing I can think of to serve you—you must strum out something—it will be a good thing for you, you know.'

'Well,' said I, 'if Mr. Yates will promise to sing nothing faster than "Je-ru-sa-lem my hap-py home," I'll accompany him.'

No—he would not be laughed out of it: he was determined to put money in my pocket, and would take no denial. 'Next Monday you will have the goodness to meet me at the theatre at six o'clock with your fiddle. Play how you like, play inaudible for what I care, but play and draw your weekly salary you must and shall.'

'Play inaudible'—these words sunk to the very bottom of me. 'Play inaudible.'

I fell into a brown study : it lasted three days and three nights; finally, to my good patron's great content, I consented to come up to the scratch : and Monday night I had the hardihood to present myself in the music-room of the Adelphi: my violin was a ringing one, I tuned up the loudest of them all, and Mr. Chaplin's eye rested on me with an approving glance.

Time was called : we played an overture, and accompanied Mr. Yates in his recitatives and songs, and performed pieces and airs between the acts &c. The leader's eye often fell on me, and, when it did, he saw the most conscientious workman of the crew ploughing every note with singular care and diligence.

In this same little orchestra was James Bates another favourite of Mr. Chaplin and an experienced fiddler.

This young man was a great chum of mine. He was a fine honest young fellow, but of rather a saturnine temper ; he was not moveable to mirth at any price. He would play without a smile to a new pantomime—stuck there all night like Solomon cut in black marble with a white choker, as solemn as a tomb with hundreds laughing all around.

Once or twice while we were at work I saw Mr. Chaplin look at Bates, knowing we two were chums, and whenever he did it seems the young one bit his lips and turned as red as a beetroot. After the lights were out Mr. Chaplin congratulated me before Bates. 'There, you see, it is not so very hard, why hang me if you did not saw away as well as the best!!!' At these words Bates gave a sort of yell and ran home. Mr. Chaplin looked after him with surprise. 'There's some devil's delight up between you two' said he. 'I shall find it out.'

Next night in the tuning-room my fiddle was so resinant it attracted attention, and one or two asked leave to try it. 'Why not?' said I.

During work Mr. Chaplin had one eye on me, and one on Bates, and caught the perspiration running down my face, and him simpering for the first time in the history of the Adelphi.

'What has come over Jem Bates?' said Mr. Chaplin to me; 'the lad is all changed: you have put some of your late gunpowder into him—there is something up between you two.' After the play he got us together and he looked Bates in the face and just said to him—'Eh?'

At this wholesale interrogatory Bates laid hold of himself tight. 'No, Mr. Chaplin sir, I can't; it will kill me when it does come out of me.'

'When what comes out? You young rascals if you don't both of you tell me I'll break my fiddle over Bates, and Jack shall mend it free of expense gratis for nothing, that is how I'll serve mutineers: come, out with it.'

'Tell him John,' said Bates, demurely.

'No,' said I, 'tell him yourself if you think it will gratify him.' I had my doubts.

'Well' said Bates, 'it is ungrateful to keep you out of it sir—so—he! he !—I'll tell you sir—this second violin has two bows in his violin-case.'

'Well stupid, what is commoner than that for a fiddler?'

'But this is not a fiddler' squeaked Bates, ' he's only a bower. Oh oh oh.'

'Only a bower?'

'No! Oh! Oh! I shall die, it will kill me.' I gave a sort of ghastly grin myself.

'You unconscionable scoundrels,' shouted Mr. Chaplin, 'there look at this Bates, he is at it again, a fellow that the very clown could never raise a laugh out of, and now I see him all night smirking and grinning and looking down like a jackdaw that has got his claw on a thimble. If you don't speak out, I'll knock your two tormenting skulls together till they

roll off down the gutter side by side, chuck-
ling and giggling all day and all night.' At
this direful mysterious threat Bates composed
himself. 'The power is all out of my body sir,
so now I can tell you.'

He then in faint tones gave this explanation, which my guilty looks confirmed. 'One
of his bows is resined sir—that one is the
tuner. I don't know whether you have observed, but he tunes rather louder than any
two of *us*. Oh dear it is coming again.'

'Don't be a fool now. Yes I have noticed
that.'

'The other bow, Mr. Chaplin sir, the other
bow is soaped, well soaped sir, for orchestral
use. Ugh. Ugh.'

'Oh the varmint!'

Bates continued. 'You take a look at him
—you see him fingering and bowing like mad
—but as for sound, you know what a greasy
bow is?'

'Of course I do. I don't wonder at your

laughing—ha ha ha. Oh the thief—when I think of his diligent face and him shaking his right wrist like Viotti.'

'Mind your pockets though—he knows too much.'

It was now my turn to speak. 'I am glad you like the idea sir,' said I, ' for it comes from you.'

'How can you say that?'

'What did you tell me to do?'

'I didn't tell you to do that. I don't remember what I told him, Bates—not to the letter.'

'Told me to play inaudible!!!'

'Well I never,' said Mr. Chaplin.

'Those were your words sir, they did not fall to the ground you see.'

My position in this orchestra and the situations that arose out of it were meat and drink to my two friends. With the gentry, whose lives are a succession of amusements, a joke soon wears out no doubt; but we poor fellows can't let one go cheap. How do we know how long it may be before Heaven sends us another? A joke falling among us is like a rat in a kennel of terriers.

At intricate passages the first violin used to look at the tenor and then at me, and wink, and they both swelled with innocent enjoyment, till at last unknown powers of gaiety budded in Bates : with quizzing his friend he learned to take a jest ; so much so that one night Mr. Yates being funnier than usual if possible, a single horse-laugh suddenly exploded among the fiddles. This was Bates gone off all in a moment after his trigger being pulled so many years to no purpose. Mr. Yates looked down with gratified surprise.

'Hallo! Brains got in the orchestra—after that anything!'

But do you think it was fun to me all this? I declare I suffered the torture of the—you know what. I never felt safe a moment. I had placed myself next to an old fiddler who was deaf, but he somehow smelt at times that I was shirking, and then he used to cry, 'pull out—pull out—you don't pull out.'

'How can you say so?' I used to reply, and then saw away like mad: when, so connected are the senses of sight and hearing apparently, the old fellow used to smile and be at peace. He saw me pull, and so he heard me pull out. Then sometimes friends of the other performers would be in the orchestra, and peep over me and say civil things and I wish them further, civilities and all. But it is a fact that for two months I gesticulated in that orchestra without a soul finding out that I was not suiting the note to the action.

At last we broke up to my great relief, but I did not leave the theatre. Mr. Widger, Mr. Yates' dresser, got me a place behind the scenes at nine shillings per week.

I used to dress Mr. Reeve and run for his

brandies and waters, which kept me on the trot, and do odd jobs.

But I was now to make the acquaintance that coloured all my life, or the cream of it. My time was come to move in a wider circle of men and things, and really to do what so many fancy they have done—to see the world.

In the month of April, 1828, Mr. Yates, theatrical manager, found his nightly receipts fall below his nightly expenses. In this situation a manager falls upon one of two things; a spectacle or a star. Mr. Yates preferred the latter, and went over to Paris and engaged Mademoiselle Djek.

Mademoiselle Djek was an elephant of great size, and unparalleled sagacity. She had been for some time performing in a play at Franconi's, and created a great sensation in Paris.

Of her previous history little is known. But she was first landed from the East in

England, and was shown about merely as an elephant by her proprietor, an Italian called Polito. The Frenchmen first found out her talent. Her present owner was a M. Huguet, and with him Mr. Yates treated. She joined the Adelphi company at a salary of £40 a-week and her grub.

There was great expectation in the theatre for some days; the play in which she was to perform "The Elephant of the King of Siam," was cast and rehearsed several times; a wooden house was built for her at the back of the stage, and one fine afternoon sure enough she arrived with all her train, one or two of each nation, viz., her owner, M. Huguet (French), her principal keeper, Tom Elliot (English), her subordinates—Bernard, (French) and an Italian nicknamed Pippin. She arrived at the stage-door in Maiden Lane, and soon after the messenger was sent to Mr. Yates's house.

'Elephant's come, sir.'

'Well, let them put her in the place built for her, and I'll come and see her.'

'They can't do that, sir.'

'Why not?'

'La bless you, sir, she might get her foot into the theatre : but how is her body to come through the stage-door? why she is almost as big as the house.'

Down comes Mr. Yates, and there was the elephant standing all across Maiden Lane— all traffic interrupted except what could pass under her belly—and such a crowd—my eye!

Mr. Yates put his hands in his pockets and took a quiet look at the state of affairs.

'You must make a hole in the wall,' said he.

Pickaxes went to work and made a hole or rather a frightful chasm in the theatre, and when it looked about two-thirds her size, Elliot said 'Stop!' He then gave her a sharp order, and the first specimen we saw of her cleverness was her doubling herself together and creeping in through that hole bending her fore-knees, and afterwards rising and dragging her hind-legs horizontally, and so she disappeared like an enormous mole burrowing into the theatre.

Mademoiselle Djek's bills were posted all over the town, and everything done to make her take, and on the following Tuesday the theatre was pretty well filled by the public: the manager also took care to have a strong party in the pit. In short, she was nursed as other stars are upon their *début*.

Night came: all was anxiety behind the lights and expectation in front.

The green curtain drew up, and Mr. Yates walked on in black dress-coat and white kid gloves, like a private gentleman just landed out of a bandbox at the Queen's ball. He was the boy to talk to the public: soft sawder —dignified reproach—friendly intercourse—he had them all at his fingers' ends. This time it was the easy tone of refined conversation upon the intelligent creature he was privileged to introduce to them. I remember his discourse as well as if it was yesterday.

'The elephant,' said Mr. Yates, 'is a marvel of Nature. We are now to have the pleasure of showing her to you as taking her place in art.' Then he praised the wisdom and beneficence of creation. 'Among the small animals, such as cats and men, there is to be found such a thing as spite; treachery ditto, and love of mischief, and even cruelty at odd times: but here is a creature with the power to pull down our houses about our ears like Samson, but a heart that will not let her hurt a fly. Properly to appreciate her moral character consider what a thing power is, see how it tries us, how often in history it has turned men to demons. The elephant,' added he, 'is the friend of man by choice, not by necessity or instinct: it is born as wild as a lion or buffalo, but the moment an oppor-

tunity arrives, its kindred intelligence allies it
to man, its only superior or equal in reasoning
power. We are about,' said Mr. Yates, ' to
present a play in which an elephant will act
a part, and yet act but herself, for the intelligence and affectionate disposition she will display on these boards as an actress are merely
her own private and domestic qualities. Not
every one of us actors, gentlemen, can say as
much.'

Then there was a laugh in which Mr.
Yates joined. In short Mr. Yates who could
play upon the public ear better than some
fiddles (I name no names) made his *débutante* popular before ever she stepped upon
the scene. He then bowed with intense gratitude to the audience for the attention they
had honoured him with, retired to the
prompter's side, and, as he reached it, the act
drop flew up and the play began : it com-
menced on two legs : the elephant did not
come on until the second scene of the act.

The drama was a good specimen of its kind: it was a story of some interest and length and variety, and the writer had been sharp enough not to make the elephant too common in it; she came on only three or four times, and always at a nick of time, and to do good business—as theatricals say, *i. e.*, for some important purpose in the story.

A king of Siam had lately died, and the elephant was seen taking her part in the funeral obsequies. She deposited his sceptre &c. in the tomb of his fathers, and was seen no more in that act. The rightful heir to this throne was a young prince to whom the elephant belonged. An usurper opposed him and a battle took place, the rightful heir was worsted and taken prisoner, the usurper condemned him to be thrown into the sea. In the next act, this sentence was being executed: four men were discovered passing through a wood carrying no end of a box. Suddenly a terrific roar was heard, the men put down the box rather more carefully than they would in real life, and fled, and the elephant walked on to the scene alone like any other actress. She smelt about the box, and presently tore it open with her proboscis, and there was her master, the rightful heir, but in a sad exhausted state. When the good soul sees this what does she do but walk to the other side and tear down the bough of a fruit-tree and hand it to the sufferer : he sucked it, and it had the effect of stout on him—it made a man of him, and they marched away together, the elephant trumpeting to show her satisfaction.

In the next act the rightful heir's friends were discovered behind the bars of a prison at a height from the ground. The order for their execution arrived, and they were down upon their luck terribly. In marched the elephant, tore out the iron bars, and squeezed herself against the wall half-squatting in the shape of a triangle : so then the prisoners glided down her to the ground slantendicular one after another.

When the civil war had lasted long enough to sicken both sides, and enough widows and orphans had been made, the Siamese began to ask themselves but what is it all about? the next thing was they said, ' What asses we have been ! was there no other way of deciding between two men but bleeding the whole tribe—then they reflected and said we are asses that is clear—but we hear there is one animal in the nation that is not an ass : why of course then she is the one to decide our dispute. Accordingly a grand assembly was held, the rival claimants were compelled to attend, and the elephant was led in. Then the high priest, or some such article, having first implored Heaven to speak through the quadruped bade her decide according to justice. No sooner were the words out of his mouth than the elephant stretched out her proboscis, seized a little crown that glittered

on the usurper's head, and waving it gracefully
in the air deposited it gently and carefully on
the brows of the rightful heir. So then there
was a rush made on the wrongful heir, he was
taken out guarded and warned off the premises: the rightful heir mounted the throne
and grinned and bowed all round—the elephant trumpeted — Siam hurrahed — Djek's
party in the house echoed the sound, and down
came the curtain in thunders of applause.
Though the curtain was down the applause
continued most vehemently, and after awhile
a cry arose at the back of the pit, 'Elephant!
Elephant!' That part of the audience that
had paid at the door laughed at this, but their
laughter turned to curiosity when in answer to
the cry the curtain was raised, and the stage
discovered empty. Curiosity in turn gave
way to surprise; for the elephant walked on
from the third grooves alone, and came slap
down to the float. At this, the astonished
public literally roared at her. But how can I

describe the effect, the amazement, when, in return for the compliment, the *débutante* slowly bent her knees and curtseyed twice to the British public, and then retired backwards as the curtain once more fell? People looked at one another and seemed to need to read in their neighbour's eyes whether such a thing was real; and then followed that buzz which tells the knowing ones behind the curtain that the nail has gone home, that the theatre will be crammed to the ceiling to-morrow night, and perhaps for eighty nights after.

Mr. Yates fed Mademoiselle Djek with his own hand that night, crying, 'Oh you duck!'

The fortunes of the Adelphi rose from that hour—full houses without intermission.

Mr. Yates shortened his introductory address, and used to make it a brief, neat, and. I think, elegant eulogy of her gentleness and affectionate disposition; her talent 'the public are here to judge for themselves,' said Mr. Yates, and exit P. S.

A theatre is a little world; and Djek soon
became the hero of ours. Everybody must
have a passing peep at the star that was
keeping the theatre open all summer, and pro-
viding bread for a score or two of families
connected with it. Of course a mind like
mine was not among the least inquisitive.
But her head-keeper Tom Elliot, a surly fellow,
repulsed our attempts to scrape acquaintance.
'Mind your business, and I'll mind mine,' was
his chant. He seemed to be wonderfully
jealous of her. He could not forbid Mr. Yates
to visit her, as he did us, but he always insisted
on being one of the party even then. He
puzzled us: but the strongest impression he
gave us was that he was jealous of her;
afraid she would get as fond of some others as
of him, and so another man might be able to
work her, and his own nose lose a joint as the
saying is; later on we learned to put a different interpretation on his conduct. Pippin
the Italian, and Bernard the Frenchman, used

to serve her with straw and water &c., but it was quite a different thing from Elliot. They were like a fine lady's grooms and running footmen, but Elliot was her body-servant, groom of the bed-chamber, or what not. He used always to sleep in the straw close to her: sometimes, when he was drunk, he would roll in between her legs, and if she had not been more careful of him than any other animal ever was (especially himself) she must have crushed him to death three nights in the week. Next to Elliot, but a long way below him, M. Huguet seemed her favourite. He used to come into her box and caress her and feed her and make much of her: but she never went on the stage without Elliot in sight, and in point of fact all she did upon our stage was done at a word of command given then and there at the side by this man and no other—going down to the float—curtseying and all.

Being mightily curious to know how he had

gained such influence with her, I made several attempts to sound him, but drunk or sober he was equally unfathomable on this point.

I then endeavoured to slake my curiosity at No. 2. I made bold to ask M. Huguet how he had won her affections. The Frenchman was as communicative as the native was reserved: he broke plenty of English over me: it came to this, that the strongest feeling of an elephant was gratitude, and that he had worked on this for years; was always kind to her and seldom approached her without giving her lumps of sugar—carried a pocket full on purpose. This tallied with what I had heard and read of an elephant: still the problem remained why is she fonder still of this Tom Elliot whose manner is not ingratiating and who never speaks to her but in a harsh severe voice.

She stood my friend any way: a good many new supers were engaged to play with her, and I was set over these, looked out their

dresses and went on with them and her as a
slave : nine shillings a week for this was
added to my other nine which I drew for
dressing an actor or two of the higher class.

The more I was about her the more I felt
that we were not at the bottom of this quadruped, nor even of her bipeds.   There were
gestures and glances and shrugs always passing to and fro among them.

One day at the rehearsal of a farce there
was no Mr. Yates.   Somebody inquired loudly
for him.

'Hush,' says another—'haven't you heard?'
'No.'
'You mustn't talk of it out of doors.'
'No!'
'Half killed by the elephant this morning.'

It seems he was feeding and coaxing her
as he had often done before, when all in a
moment she laid hold of him with her trunk
and gave him a squeeze.   He lay in bed six
weeks with it, and there was nobody to

deliver her eulogy at night. Elliot was at the other end of the stage when the accident happened: he heard Mr. Yates cry out, and ran in, and the elephant let Mr. Yates go the moment she saw him.

We questioned Elliot. We might as well have cross-examined the Monument. Then I inquired of M. Huguet what this meant. That gentleman explained to me that Djek had miscalculated her strength, that she wanted to caress so kind a manager who was always feeding and courting her, and had embraced him too warmly.

The play went on and the elephant's reputation increased. But her popularity was destined to receive a shock as far as we little ones behind the curtain were concerned.

One day, while Pippin was spreading her straw, she knocked him down with her trunk, and pressing her tooth against him, bored two frightful holes in his skull, before Elliot could interfere. Pippin was carried to St. George's

Hospital, and we began to look in one another's faces.

Pippin's situation was in the market.

One or two declined it—it came down to me —I reflected, and accepted it—another nine shillings, total twenty-seven shillings.

That night two supers turned tail. An actress also, whose name I have forgotten, refused to go on with her. 'I was not engaged to play with a brute,' said this lady, ' and I won't; ' others went on as usual, but were not so sweet on it as before. The rightful heir lost all relish for his part, and above all, when his turn came to be preserved from harm by her, I used to hear him crying out of the box to Elliot 'Are you there? are you sure you are there?' and, when she tore open his box, Garrick never acted better than this one used to now; for you see his cue was to exhibit fear and exhaustion, and he did both to the life, because for the last five minutes he had been thinking—'Oh dear!

oh dear! suppose she should do the foot business on my box, instead of the proboscis business.'

These however were vain fears: she made no mistake before the public.

Nothing lasts for ever in this world, and the time came that she ceased to fill the house. Then Mr. Yates re-engaged her for the provinces, and, having agreed with the country managers, sent her down to Bath and Bristol first. He had a good opinion of me and asked me to go with her and watch his interests. I should not certainly have applied for the place, but it was not easy to say no to Mr. Yates, and I felt I owed him some reparation for the wrong I had done that great artist in accompanying his voice with my gestures.

In short we started, Djek, Elliot, Bernard, I, and Pippin, on foot (he was just out of St. George's). Messrs. Huguet and Yates rolled in their carriage to meet us at the principal towns where we played.

As we could not afford to make her common, our walking was all nightwork and introduced me to a rough life.

The average of night weather is wetter and windier than day, and many a vile night we tramped through when wise men were abed; and we never knew for certain where we should pass the night: for it depended on Djek. She was so enormous that half the inns could not find us a place big enough for her. Our first evening stroll was to Bath and Bristol: thence we crossed to Dublin, thence we returned to Plymouth. We walked from Plymouth to Liverpool, playing with good success at all these places. At Liverpool she laid hold of Bernard and would have settled his hash, but Elliot came between them.

That same afternoon in walks a young gentleman dressed in the height of Parisian fashion—glossy hat, satin tie, trousers puckered at the haunches—sprucer than any poor Englishman will be while the world lasts, and who was it but Mons. Bernard come to take leave. We endeavoured to dissuade him: he smiled and shook his head, treated us, flattered us, and showed us his preparations for France.

All that day and the next he sauntered about us, dressed like a gentleman, with his hands in his pockets and an ostentatious neglect of his late affectionate charge. Before he left he invited me to drink something at his expense, and was good enough to say I was what he most regretted leaving.

'Then why go?' said I.

'I will tell you, mon pauvre garçon,' said Mons. Bernard. 'We old hands have all got our orders to say she is a duck. Ah, you have found that out of yourself. Well now, as I have done with her, I will tell you a part of her character, for I know her well. Once she injures you she can never forgive you. So long as she has never hurt you there's a fair chance she never will. I have been about her for years, and she never molested me till yesterday. But—if she once attacks a man, that man's death-warrant is signed—I can't altogether account for it: but trust my experience it is so. I would have stayed with you all my life if she had not shown me my fate; but not now: merci! I have a wife and two children in France. I have saved some money out of her: I return to the bosom of my family: and if Pippin stays with her after the hint she gave him in London, why you will see the death of Pippin, my lad, voilà tout, that is if you don't go first. Qu'est que ça te fait à la fin? tu es garçon toi—buvons!

The next day he left us, and left me sad for one. The quiet determination with which he acted upon positive experience of her was enough to make a man thoughtful. And then Bernard was the flower of us: he was the drop of mirth and gaiety in our iron cup. He was a pure unadulterated Frenchman, and to be just—where can you find anything so delightful as a Frenchman—. Of the right sort?

He fluttered home singing

‘ Les doux yeux de ma brunet—te,
   Tout—e mignonett—e—tout—e gentillett—e,’

and left us all in black.

God bless you my merry fellow. I hope
you found your children healthy, and your
brunette true, and your friends alive, and that
the world is just to you, and smiles on you, as
you do on it, and did on us.

From Liverpool we walked to Glasgow:
from Glasgow to Edinburgh: and from Edinburgh on a cold starry midnight we started for
Newcastle.

In this interval of business let me paint
you my companions Pippin and Elliot. The
reader is entitled to this, for there must have
been something out of the common in their
looks, since I was within an ace of being
killed along of the Italian’s face, and was
imprisoned four days through the Englishman’s
mug.

The Italian whom we know by the nick-

name of Pippin was a man of immense
stature and athletic mould.   His face, once
seen, would never be forgotten.   His skin,
almost as swarthy as Othello's, was set off
by dazzling ivory teeth, and lighted by two
glorious large eyes, black as jet, brilliant as
diamonds : the orbs of black lightning gleamed
from beneath eyebrows that many a dandy
would have bought for moustaches at a high
valuation.   A nose like a reaping-hook com-
pleted him—perch him on a tolerable-sized
rock and there you had a black eagle.

As if this was not enough, Pippin would
always wear a conical hat, and had he but
stepped upon the stage in " Massaniello " or the
like, all the other brigands would have sunk
down to rural police by the side of our man.
But now comes the absurdity : his inside was
not different from his out, it was the exact
opposite.   You might turn over twenty thousand bullet heads and bolus eyes, before you
could find one man so thoroughly harmless as

this thundering brigand. He was just a pet, an universal pet of all the men and women that came near him. He had the disposition of a dove and the heart of a hare. He was a lamb in wolf's clothing.

My next portrait is not so pleasing.

A MAN TURNED BRUTE.

Some ten years before this, a fine stout young English rustic entered the service of Mademoiselle Djek. He was a model for bone and muscle, and had two cheeks like roses: when he first went to Paris he was looked on as a curiosity there. People used to come to Djek's stable to see her, and Elliot the young English Samson. Just ten years after this young Elliot had got to be called 'old Elliot.' His face was not only pale it was colourless: it was the face of a walking corpse. This came of ten years' brandy and brute. I have often asked people to guess the man's age, and they always guessed sixty sixty-five or seventy oftenest the latter.

He was thirty-five, not a day more.

This man's mind had come down along with his body. He understood nothing but elephant, he seldom talked, and then nothing but elephant. He was an elephant-man. I will give you an instance which I always thought curious.

An elephant, you may have observed, cannot stand quite still. The great weight of its head causes a nodding movement, which is perpetual when the creature stands erect. Well, this Tom Elliot, when he stood up, used always to have one foot advanced, and his eye half closed, and his head niddle noddling like an elephant all the time; and with it all such a presence of brute and absence of soul in his mug, enough to give a thoughtful man some very queer ideas about man and beast.

CHAPTER VI.

My office in this trip was merely to contract for the elephant's food at the various places; but I was getting older and shrewder, and more designing than I used to be, and I was quite keen enough to see in this elephant the means of bettering my fortunes if I could but make friends with her. But how to do this? She was like a coquette: strange admirers welcome; but when you had courted her a while she got tired of you, and then nothing short of your demise satisfied her caprice. Her heart seemed inaccessible, except to this brute Elliot, and he, drunk or sober, guarded the secret of his fascination by some instinct; for reason he possessed in a very small degree.

I played the spy on quadruped and biped, and I found out the fact but the reason beat me. I saw that she was more tenderly careful of him than a mother of her child. I saw him roll down stupid drunk under her belly, and I saw her lift first one foot and then the other, and draw them slowly and carefully back, trembling with fear lest she might make a mistake and hurt him.

But why she was a mother to him, and a step-mother to the rest of us, that I could not learn.

One day between Plymouth and Liverpool having left Elliot and her together, I happened to return and I found the elephant alone and in a state of excitement, and looking in I observed some blood upon the straw

His turn has come at last was my first

notion ; but looking round there was Elliot behind me.

'I was afraid she had tried it on with you,' I said.

'Who?'

'The elephant.'

Elliot's face was not generally expressive, but the look of silent scorn he gave me at the idea of the elephant attacking him was worth seeing. The brute knew something I did not know, and could not find out; and from this one piece of knowledge he looked down upon me with a sort of contempt that set all the Seven Dials' blood on fire.

'I will bottom this,' said I, 'if I die for it.'

My plan now was to feed Djek every day with my own hand, but never to go near her without Elliot at my very side and in front of the elephant.

This was my first step.

We were now drawing towards Newcastle,

and had to lie at Morpeth; where we arrived
late, and found Mr. Yates and M. Huguet,
who had come out from Newcastle to meet
us: and at this place I determined on a new
move which I had long meditated.

Elliot, I reflected, always slept with the
elephant. None of the other men had ever
done this. Now might there not be some
magic in this unbroken familiarity between
the two animals?

Accordingly at Morpeth I pretended there
was no bed vacant in the inn, and asked Elliot
to let me lie beside him: he grunted an un-
gracious assent.

Not to overdo it at first, I got Elliot between
me and Djek, so that if she was offended at my
intrusion, she must pass over her darling to
resent it: we had tramped a good many miles
and were soon fast asleep.

About two in the morning, I was awoke by
a shout and a crunching, and felt myself
dropping into the straw out of the elephant's

mouth. She had stretched her proboscis over him—had taken me up so delicately that I felt nothing, and when Elliot shouted I was in her mouth; at his voice, that rang in my ears like the last trumpet, she dropped me like a hot potato. I rolled out of the straw giving tongue a good one, and ran out of the shed. I had no sooner got to the inn than I felt a sickening pain in my shoulder and fainted away.

Her huge tooth had gone into my shoulder like a wedge. It was myself I had heard being crunched.

They did what they could for me and I soon came to. When I recovered my senses I was seized with vomiting: but at last all violent symptoms abated; and I began to suffer great pain in the injured part, and did suffer for six weeks.

And so I scraped clear. Somehow or other Elliot was not drunk, or nothing could have saved me: for a second wonder he, who was a heavy sleeper, woke at the very slight noise she made eating me; a moment later and nothing could have saved me. I use too many words—suppose she had eaten me—what then?

They told Mr. Yates at breakfast, and he sent for me and advised me to lie quiet at Morpeth till the fever of the wound should be off me; but I refused. She was to start at ten and I told him I should start with her.

Running from grim death like that I had left my shoes behind in the shed, and M. Huguet sent his servant Baptiste, an Italian, for them.

Mr. Yates then asked me for all the particulars, and whilst I was telling him and M. Huguet, we heard a commotion in the street, and saw people running, and presently one of the waiters ran in and cried,

'The elephant has killed a man or near it.'

Mr. Yates laughed and said

'Not quite so bad as that; for here is the man.'

'No, no.!' cried the waiter, 'it is not him; it is one of the foreigners.'

Mr. Yates started up all trembling: he ran to the stable: I followed him as I was, and there we saw a sight to make our blood run cold. On the corn-bin lay poor Baptiste crushed into a mummy. How it happened there was no means of knowing—but, no doubt, while he was groping in the straw for my wretched shoes, she struck him with her trunk, perhaps more than once,—his breast-bones were broken to chips, and every time he breathed, which by God's mercy was not many minutes, the man's whole chest frame puffed out like a bladder with the action of his lungs—it was too horrible to look at.

Elliot had run at Baptiste's cry, but too late to save his life this time. He had drawn the man out of the straw as she was about to pound him to a jelly, and there the poor soul lay on the corn-bin, and by his side lay the things he had died for; two old shoes. Elliot had found them in the straw and put them there of all places in the world.

By this time all Morpeth was out. They besieged the doors and vowed death to the elephant. M. Huguet became greatly alarmed: he could spare Baptiste but he could not spare Djek. He got Mr. Yates to pacify the people —'tell them something,' said he.

'What on earth can I say for her over that man's bleeding body?' said Mr. Yates. 'Curse her! would to God I had never seen her!'

'Tell them he used her cruel,' said M. Huguet, 'I have brought her off with that before now.'

Well my sickness came on again, partly no doubt by the sight and the remorse, and I was got to bed and lay there some days; so I did not see all that passed, but I heard some and I know the rest by instinct now.

Half an hour after breakfast-time Baptiste died. On this the elephant was detained by the authorities, and a coroner's inquest was summoned, and sat in the shambles on the victim, with the butcheress looking on at the proceedings.

Pippin told me she took off a juryman's hat during the investigation, waved it triumphantly in the air, and placed it cleverly on her favourite's head old Tom.

At this inquest two or three persons deposed on oath that the deceased had ill used her more than once in France, in particular that he had run a pitchfork into her two years ago, that he had been remonstrated with but in vain; unfortunately she had recognised him at once, and killed him out of revenge for past cruelty, or to save herself from fresh outrages.

This cooled the ardour against her. Some even took part with her against the man.

'Run a pitchfork into an elephant! Oh for

shame! no wonder she killed him at last. How good of her not to kill him then and there—what forbearance—forgave it for two years, ye see.'

There is a fixed opinion among men that an elephant is a good kind creature; the opinion is fed by the proprietors of elephants, who must nurse the notion or lose their customers, and so a set tale is always ready to clear the guilty and criminate the sufferer; and this tale is greedily swallowed by the public. You will hear and read many such tales in the papers before you die. Every such tale is a lie.

How curiously things happen! Last year *i. e.*, more than twenty years after this event, my little girl went for a pound of butter to Newport Street. She brought it wrapped up in a scrap of a very old newspaper; in unrolling it, my eye by mere accident fell upon these words 'An inquest.' I had no sooner read the paragraph than I put the scrap of paper away in my desk : it lies before me now, and I am copying it.

'An inquest was held at the Phœnix Inn
'Morpeth on the 27th ultimo, on view of
'the body of an Italian named Baptiste
'Bernard, who was one of the attendants
'on the female elephant which lately
'performed at the Adelphi. It appeared
'from the evidence that the man had
'stabbed the elephant in the trunk with a
'pitchfork about two years ago while in
'a state of intoxication, and that on
'the Tuesday previous to the inquest,
'the animal caught hold of him with
'her trunk, and did him so much injury
'that he died in a few hours. Verdict
'died from the wounds and bruises
'received from the trunk of an elephant.
'Deodand 5s."

Well this has gone all abroad : for print travels like wind : and it is not fair to the friends and the memory of this Baptiste

M

Bernard to print that he died by his own cruelty, or fault, or folly

So take my deposition, and carry it to Milan, his native city.

I declare upon oath that the above is a lie. That the man was never an attendant upon the female elephant; he was an attendant on the female Huguet. For he was that lady's footman. His first introduction to Mademoiselle Djek was her killing him, and he died, not by any fault of his own, but by the will of God and through ignorance of the real nature of the *full-grown elephant*, the cunningest, most treacherous, and blood-thirsty beast that ever played the butcher among mankind.

What men speak dissolves in the air, what they print stands fast and will look them in the face to all eternity. I print the truth about this man's death so help me God.

Business is business. As soon as we had got the inquest over and stamped the lie current, hid the truth and buried the man, we marched south and played our little play at Newcastle.

Deodand for a human soul sent by murder to its account, five bob.

After Newcastle we walked to York and thence to Manchester. I crept along thoroughly crestfallen. Months and months I had watched and spied and tried to pluck out the heart of this Tom Elliot's mystery I had failed—months and months I had tried to gain some influence over Djek. I had failed—but for Elliot it was clear I should not live a single day within reach of her trunk, this brute was my superior. I was compelled to look up to him, and I *did look up to him*.

As I tramped sulkily along my smarting shoulder reminded me that in elephant, as in everything else I had tried, I was Jack, not master.

The proprietors had their cause of discontent too; we had silenced the law but we could not silence opinion. Somehow suspicion

hung about her in the very air wherever she
went.   She never throve in the English
provinces after the Morpeth job, and finding
this, Mr. Yates said, 'Oh hang her, she has
lost her character here.   Send her to America.'
So he and M. Huguet joined partnership and
took this new speculation on their shoulders.
America was even in that day a great card if
you went with an English or French reputation.

I had been thinking of leaving her and her
old Tom in despair; but now that other
dangers and inconveniences were to be
endured besides her and her trunk, by some
strange freak of human nature, or by fate, I
began to cling to her like a limpet to a rock
the more you pull at him.

Mr. Yates dissuaded me. 'Have nothing to
do with her, Jack.   She will serve you like all
the rest.   Stay at home and I'll find something for you in the theatre.'

I thought a great deal of Mr. Yates for

this . for he was speaking against his own interest. I was a faithful servant to him and he needed one about her. Many a five-pound note I had saved him already, and well he deserved it at my hands.

'No sir,' I said, 'I shall be of use and I can't bear to be nonplushed by two brutes like Elliot and her. I have begun to study her and I must go on to the word "finis!"'

Messrs. Yates and Huguet ensured the elephant for £20,000, and sent us all to sea together in the middle of November, a pretty month to cross the Atlantic in.

This was what betters call a hedge; and not a bad one.

Our party was Queen Djek, Mr. Stevenson her financier, Mr. Gallott her stage-manager and wrongful heir; Elliot her keeper, her lord, her king; Pippin her slave always trembling for his head, myself her commissariat, and one George Hinde from Wombwell's her man-of-all-work.

She had a stout cabin built upon deck for her. It cost £40 to make; what she paid for the accommodation heaven knows, but I should think a good round sum, for it was the curse of the sailors and passengers and added fresh terrors to navigation; the steersman could not see the ship's head, until the sea took the mariners' part and knocked it into toothpicks.

Captain Sebor had such a passage with us as he had never encountered before; he told us so—and no wonder; he never had such a wholesale murderess on board before,—contrary winds for ever and stiff gales too. At last it blew great guns; and one night as the sun went down crimson in the Gulf of Florida, the sea running mountains high, I saw Captain Sebor himself was fidgety. He had cause: that night a tempest came on : " the Ontario " rolled fearfully and groaned like a dying man; about two in the morning a sea struck her, smashed Djek's cabin to atoms and left her exposed and reeling; another such would now have swept her overboard, but her wits never left her for a moment. She threw herself down flatter than any man could have conceived possible; out went all her four legs and she glued her belly to the deck: the sailors passed a chain from the weather to the lee bulwarks, and she seized it with her proboscis, and held on like grim death. Poor thing her coat never got not to say dry—she was like a great water-rat all the rest of the voyage.

The passage was twelve weeks of foul weather; the elephant began to be suspected of being the cause of this, and the sailors often looked askaunt at her, and said we should never see port till she walked the plank into the Atlantic. If her underwriters saved their twenty thousand pounds it was touch and go more than once or twice. Moreover she ate so little all the voyage that it was a wonder to Elliot and me how she came not to die of sickness and hunger. I suppose she survived it all because she had more mischief to do.

As the pretty little witches sing in Mr. Locke's opera of " Macbeth."

She must, she must, she must, she must, she must shed—much——more——blood.

CHAPTER VII.

OUR preposterous long voyage deranged all the calculations that had been made for us in England, and we reached New York just at the wrong time. We found Master Burke playing at the Park Theatre, and we were forced to treat with an inferior house, the Bowery Theatre. We played there with but small success compared with what we had been used to in Europe. Master Burke filled the house—we did not fill ours—so that at last she was actually eclipsed by a human actor: to be sure it was a boy, not a man, and child's play is sometimes preferred by the theatre-going world even to horse-play.

The statesmen were cold to us; they had not at this time learned to form an opinion of their own at sight on such matters, and we did not bring them an overpowering European verdict to which they had nothing to do but sign their names. There was no groove cut for the mind to run in, and while they hesitated, the speculation halted. I think she would succeed there now; but at this time they were not ripe for an elephant.

We left New York and away to Philadelphia on foot and steamboat.

There is a place on the Delaware where the boat draws up to a small pier. Down this we marched, and about ten yards from the end the floor gave way under her weight and Djek and her train fell into the sea. I was awoke from a reverie and found myself sitting right at top of her, with my knees in Chesapeake Bay. Elliot had a rough Benjamin on, and as he was coming thundering down with the rest of the rubbish alive and dead, it caught in a nail and he hung over the bay by the shoulder like an Indian fakeer, cursing and swearing for all the world like a dog barking : I never saw such a posture—and, oh! the language !

I swam out ; but Djek was caught in a trap between the two sets of piles. The water was about two feet over her head, so that every now and then she disappeared, and then striking the bottom she came up again, plunging and rolling and making waves like a steamboat : her trunk she kept vertical like the hose of a diving-bell, and oh, the noises that came up from the bottom of the sea through that flesh-pipe : for about four hours she went up and down the gamut of 'O Lord what shall I do?' more than a thousand times I think. We brought ropes to her aid and boats and men, and tried all we knew to move her but in vain ; and when we had exhausted our sagacity, she drew upon a better bank, her own. Talk of brutes not being able to

reason—gammon.   Djek could reason like
Solomon ; for each fresh difficulty she found
a fresh resource.   On this occasion she did
what I never saw her do before or since: she
took her enormous skull, and used it as a bat-
tering ram against the piles; two of them
resisted—no wonder—they were about eight
inches in diameter; the third snapped like
glass and she plunged through and waddled
on shore.   I met her with a bucket of brandy
and hot water—stiff.

Ladies, who are said to sip this compound
in your boudoirs while your husbands are
smoking at the clubs, but I don't believe it of
you, learn how this lady disposed of her
wooden tumbler full.   She thrust her proboscis into it.   Whis—s—s—s—p!   Now it
is all in her trunk.   Whis—s—s—sh—now it
is all in her abdomen : one breath drawn and
exhaled sent it from the bucket home.   This
done, her eye twinkled and she trumpeted to
the tune of ' All is well that ends well.'

I should weary the reader were I to relate at length all the small incidents that befel us in the United States.

The general result was failure, loss of money, our salaries not paid up, and fearful embarrassments staring us in the face; we scraped through without pawning the elephant, but we were often on the verge of it. All this did not choke my ambition. Warned by the past I never ventured near her (unless Elliot was there) for twelve months after our landing; but I was always watching Elliot and her to find the secret of his influence.

A fearful annoyance to the leaders of the speculation was the drunkenness of Old Tom and George Hinde : these two encouraged one another and defied us, and of course they were our masters, because no one but Elliot could move the elephant from place to place or work her on the stage.

One night Elliot was so drunk that he fell down senseless at the door of her shed on his way to repose. I was not near but Mr. Gallott it seems was, and he told us she put out her proboscis, drew him tenderly in, laid him on the straw, and flung some straw over him or partly over him. Mr. Gallott is alive and a public character: you can ask him whether this is true : I tell this one thing on hear-say

Not long after this, in one of the American towns, I forget which, passing by Djek's shed, I heard a tremendous row. I was about to call Elliot, thinking it was the old story, somebody getting butchered : but, I don't know how it was, something stopped me, and I looked cautiously in instead, and I saw Tom Elliot walking into her with a pitchfork — she trembling like a schoolboy with her head in a corner—and the blood streaming from her sides. As soon as he caught sight of me he left off and muttered unintelligibly. I said nothing. I thought the more.

CHAPTER VIII.

WE had to go by water to a place called City Point, and thence to Pittsville. I made a mistake as to the hour the boat started; and Djek and Co. went on board without me.

Well, you will say I could follow by the next boat. But how about the tin to pay the passage? My pocket was dry: and the treasurer gone on. But I had a good set of blacking brushes; so sold them, and followed on with the proceeds: got to City Point. Elephant gone on to Pittsville; that I expected. Twenty miles or so I had to tramp on an empty stomach. And now doesn't the devil send me a fellow who shows me a short cut through a wood to Pittsville: into the wood I go. I thought it was to be like an English wood: out of the sun into a pleasant shade, and, by then you are cool, into the world again. Instead of that, 'the deeper the deeper you are in it' as the song of the bottle says, the further you were from getting out of it. Presently two roads instead of one, and then I knew I was done. I took one road: it twisted like a serpent. I had not been half an hour on it before I lost all the points of the compass. Says I I don't know whether I ever shall see daylight again; but if I do, City Point will be the first thing I shall see. You mark my words said I.

So here was I lost in what they call a wood out there, but we should call a forest at home. And now, being in the heart of it, I got among the devilishest noises, and nothing to be seen to account for them: little feet suddenly pattering and scurrying along the ground, wings flapping out of trees; but what struck most awe into a chap from the Seven Dials was the rattle; the everlasting rattle, and nothing to show. Often I have puzzled myself what this rattle could be. It was like a thousand rattlesnakes, and didn't I wish I was in the Seven Dials, though some get lost in them for that matter. After all I think it was only insects: but insects by billions—you never heard anything like it in an English wood.

Just as I was losing heart in this enchanted wood, I heard an earthly sound, the tramp of a horse's foot. It was music.

But the leaves were so thick I could not see where the horse was: he seemed to get farther off, and then nearer. At last the sound came so close I made a run, burst through a lot of green leaves, and came out plump on a man riding a grey cob. He up with the butt-end of his whip to fell me, but seeing I was respectable, 'Hallo! stranger' says he 'guess you sort o'

N

startled me.' 'Beg pardon sir' says I, 'but I have lost my way.' 'I see you are a stranger' said he.

So then he asked me where I was bound for, and I told him—Pittsville.

I won't insult the reader by telling him what he said about the course I had been taking through the wood. I might as well tell him his A B C, or which side his bread and butter falls in the dust on. Then he asked me who I was, so I told him I was one of the elephant's domestics, leastways I did not word it so candid ; 'I was in charge of the elephant, and had taken a short cut.'

Now he had heard of Djek, and seen her bills up, so he knew it was all right. 'How am I to find my way out, sir ?' said I. 'Find your way out?' said he. 'You will never find your way out.' 'Good news, that.'

He thought a bit, then he said, 'the best thing you can do is to come home with me, and to-morrow, I will send you on.'

I could have hugged him.

You had better walk behind me, says he, my pony bites. So I tramped astern: and on we went patter, patter, patter through the wood. At first I felt as jolly as a sand-boy marching behind the pony: but when we had pattered best part of an hour, I began to have my misgivings. In all the enchanted woods ever I had read of there was a small trifle of a wizard or ogre that took you home and settled your hash. Fee faw fum, I smell the blood of an English-mun, &c.

And still on we pattered, and the sun began to decline, and the wood to darken, and still we pattered on. I was just thinking of turning tail and slipping back among the panthers and mosquitoes and rattlesnakes, when, O be joyful, we burst on a clearing, and there was a nice house in the middle of it, and out came the dogs jumping to welcome us and niggers no end, with white eyeballs and grinders like snow.

They pulled him off his horse, and in we went. There was his good lady, and his daughter a beautiful girl, and such a dinner. We sat down, and I maintained a modest taciturnity for some minutes : 'the silent hog eats the most acorns.' After dinner he shows me all manner of ways of mixing the grog, and I show him one way of drinking it—when you can get it. Then he must hear about the elephant: so I tell him the jade's history, but bind him to secresy.

Then the young lady puts in. 'So you are really an Englishman?' and she looks me all over. 'That you may take your oath of miss,' says I.

'Oh!' says she, and smiles. I did not take it up at first, but I see what it was now. Me standing five feet four, I did not come up to her notion of the Father of all Americans. 'Does this great people spring from such a little stock as we have here?' thinks my young lady. I should have up and told her the pluck makes the man and not the inches; but I lost that chance. Then being pressed with questions I told them all my adventures, and they hung on my words. It was a new leaf to them, I could see that.

The young lady her eyes glittered like two purple stars at a stranger with the gift of the gab, that had seen so much life as I had, and midnight came in no time. Then I was ushered to bed. Now up to that time I had always gone to roost without pomp or ceremony; sometimes with a mole candle, but oftener a farthing dip, which I *have* seen it dart its beams out of a bottle instead of a flat candlestick.

This time a whole cavalcade of us went up the stairs: one blackie marched in my van with two lights, two blackies brought up my rear. They showed me into a beautiful room, and stood in the half-light with eyes and teeth like red-hot silver, glittering and diabolical. I thought of course they would go away now. Not they. Presently one imp of darkness brings me a chair.

I sit down, and wonder. Other two lay hold of my boots and whip them off. This done they buzz about me like black and white fiends, fidgetting, till I longed to punch their heads. They pull my coat off and my trousers; then they hoist me into bed : this done, first one makes a run and tucks me in and grins over me diabolical : then another comes like a battering-ram, and tucks me in tighter. Fiend 3 looks at the work and puts the artful touches at the corners, and behold me wedged, and then the benefi- cent fiends mizzled with a hearty grin that seemed to turn them all ivory. I could not believe my senses : I had never been tucked in since my mother's time.

In the morning, struggled out, and came down to breakfast. Took leave of the good Samaritan, who appointed two of my niggers to see me out of the wood: made my bow to

the ladies, and away with a grateful heart.
The niggers conducted me clear of the wood
and set me on the broad road. Then came
one of the pills a poor fellow has to stomach.
I had made friends with the poor darkies, and
now I had not even a few pence to give
them, and such a little would have gone so
far with them. I have often felt the bitter-
ness of poverty, but never I do think as when
I parted with my poor niggers at the edge of
the wood, and was forced to see them go
slowly home without a farthing.

I wish these few words could travel across
the water, and my good host might read them,
and see I have not forgotten him all these
years. But, dear heart, you may be sure he
is not upon the earth now. It is years ago,
and a man that had the heart to harbour a
stranger and a wanderer, why he would be
one of the first to go.

We steamed and tramped up and down the
United States of America. On our return to

Norfolk, she broke loose at midnight, slipped into the town, took up the trees on the Boulevard and strewed them flat, went into the market, broke into a vegetable shop, munched the entire stock, next to a coach-maker's, took off a carriage-wheel, opened the door, stripped the cushions, and we found her eating the stuffing.

One day at noon, we found ourselves four-teen miles from the town, I forget its name, we had to play in that very night. Mr. Gallott had gone on to rehearse, &c., and it behoved us to be marching after him. At this juncture old Tom being rather drunk feels a strong desire to be quite drunk, and refuses to stir from his brandy-and-water. Our exchequer was in no condition to be trifled with thus: if Elliot & Co. became helpless for an hour or two we should arrive too late for the night's performance and Djek eating her head off all the while. I coaxed and threatened our two brandy sponges: but in vain: they stuck and sucked; I was in despair, and being in despair came to a desperate resolution; I determined to try and master her myself then and there and to defy these drunkards.

I told Pippin my project: he started back aghast: he viewed me in the light of a madman 'are you tired of your life?' said he. But I was inflexible. Seven Dials' pluck was up. I was enraged with my drunkards, and I was tired of waiting so many years the slave of a quadruped whose master was a brute.

Elephants are driven with a rod of steel sharpened at the end; about a foot from the end of this weapon is a large hook; by sticking this hook into an elephant's ear, and pulling it, you make her sensible which way you want her to go, and persuade her to comply.

Armed with this tool I walked up to Djek's shed and in the most harsh and brutal voice I could command, bade her come out. She moved in the shed, but hesitated. I repeated the command still more repulsively and out she came towards me very slowly.

With beasts such as lions, tigers and elephants, great promptitude is the thing. Think for them! don't give *them* time to think, or their thoughts may be evil; I had learned this much, so I introduced myself by driving the steel into Djek's ribs, and then hooking her ear, while Pippin looked down from a first story window. If Djek had known how my heart was beating she would have killed me then and there; but, observing no hesitation on my part, she took it all as a matter of course and walked with me like a lamb. I found myself alone with her on the road and fourteen miles of it before us. It was a serious situation but I was ripe for it now. All the old women's stories and traditions about an elephant's character had been driven out of me by experience and washed out with blood. I had fathomed Elliot's art. I had got what the French call the riddle-key of Mademoiselle Djek and that key was 'steel!'

On we marched the best of friends—there were a number of little hills on the road, and as we mounted one, a figure used to appear behind us on the crest of the last between us and the sky—this was the gallant Pippin, solicitous for his friend's fate, but desirous of not partaking it if adverse. And still the worthy Djek and I marched on the best of friends. About a mile out of the town she put out her trunk and tried to curl it round me in a caressing way. I met this overture by driving the steel into her till the blood squirted out of her. If I had not, the syren would have killed me in the course of the next five minutes. Whenever she relaxed her speed, I drove the steel into her. When the afternoon sun smiled gloriously on us and the poor thing felt nature stir in her heart, and began to frisk in her awful clumsy way, pounding the great globe, I drove the steel into her : if I had not, I should not be here to relate this sprightly narrative.

Meantime at —— her stage-manager and financier were in great distress and anxiety, four o'clock, and no elephant. At last they got so frightened, they came out to meet us, and presently to their amazement and delight Djek strode up with her new general. Their ecstacy was great to think the whole business was no longer at a drunkard's mercy. 'But how did you manage ? how ever did ye win her heart ? '—' With this,' said I, and showed them the bloody steel.

We had not been in the town half an hour before Tom and George came in. They were not so drunk but what they trembled for their situations after my exploit, and rolled and zigzagged after us as fast as they could.

By these means I rose from mademoiselle's slave to be her friend and companion.

CHAPTER IX.

—◆—

THIS feat kept my two drunkards in better order, and revived my own dormant ambition. I used now to visit her by myself steel in hand, to feed her, &c., and scrape acquaintance with her by every means—steel in hand. One day I was feeding her, when suddenly I thought a house had fallen on me. I felt myself crashing against the door, and there I was lying upon it in the passage with all the breath driven clean out of my body. Pippin came and lifted me up and carried me into the air. I thought I should have died before breath could get into my lungs again. She

had done this with a push from the thick end
of her proboscis. After a while I came to.
I had no sooner recovered my breath than I
ran into the stable, and came back with a
pitchfork. Pippin saw my intention and
implored me for Heaven's sake not to. I
would not listen to him—he flung his arms
round me. I threatened to turn the fork on
him if he did not let me go.

'Hark!' said he, and sure enough there she
was snorting and getting up her rage. 'I
know all about that,' said I: 'my death-
warrant is drawn up, and if I don't strike it
will be signed: this is how she has felt her
way with all of them before she has killed
them. I have but one chance of life,' said I,
'and I won't throw it away without a
struggle.' I opened the door, and, with a
mind full of misgivings I walked quickly up
to her. I did not hesitate or raise the question which of us two was to suffer; I knew
that would not do. I sprang upon her like a

tiger, and drove the pitchfork into her trunk. She gave a yell of dismay and turned a little from me; I drove the fork into her ear.

Then came out her real character.

She wheeled round, ran her head into a corner, stuck out her great buttocks and trembled all over like a leaf. I stabbed her with all my force for half an hour till the blood poured out of every square foot of her huge body, and, during the operation, she would have crept into a nut-shell if she could. I filled her as full of holes as a cloved orange.

The blood that trickled out of her saved mine: and, for the first time I walked out of her shambles her master.

One year and six months after we had landed at New York to conquer another hemisphere, we turned tail and sailed for England again. We had a prosperous voyage with the exception of one accident. George Hinde from incessant brandy had delirium tremens, and one night, in a fit of it, he had just sense enough to see that he was hardly to be trusted with the care of himself. 'John,' said he to me, 'tie me to this mast hand and foot.' I demurred: but he begged me for Heaven's sake; so I bound him hand and foot as per order. This done, some one called me down below, and whilst I was there it seems George got very uncomfortable and began to hallo and complain. Up comes the captain; sees a man lashed to the mast. 'What game is this?' says he. 'It is that little blackguard John,' says Hinde, 'he caught me sleeping against the mast and took a mean advantage: do loose me captain!' The captain made sure it was a sea-jest, and loosed him with his own hands. 'Thank you, captain,' says George, 'you are a good fellow. God bless you all!' and with these words he ran aft and jumped into the sea. A Yankee sailor made a grab at him and just touched his coat, but it was too late to save him, and we were going before the wind ten knots an hour. Thus George Hinde fell by brandy: his kindred spirit old Tom seemed ready to follow without the help of water salt or fresh. This man's face was now an uniform colour, white, with a scarce perceptible bluish yellowish tinge. He was a moving corpse.

Drink for ever! It makes men thieves, murderers, asses, and paupers; but, what about that, so long as it sends them to an early grave with 'beast' for their friends to write over their tombstones, unless they have a mind to tell lies in a churchyard, and that is a common trick.

We arrived at the mouth of the Thames.

Some boats boarded us with fresh provisions and delicacies; among the rest one I had not tasted for many a day, it is called soft-tommy at sea, and, on land, bread. The merchant stood on tip-toe and handed a loaf towards me, and I leaned over the bulwarks and stretched down to him with a shilling in my hand. But, as ill-luck would have it, the shilling slipped from my fingers and fell. If it had been some men's it would have fallen into the boat, others', into the sea, slap; but it was mine, and so it fell on the boat's very rim and then danced to its own music into the water. I looked after it in silence; a young lady, with whom I had made some little acquaintance during the voyage, happened to be at my elbow, and she laughed most merrily as the shilling went down. I remember being astonished that she laughed. The man still held out the bread : but I shook my head. 'I must go without now,' said I; the young lady was quite surprised. 'Why it is worth a guinea,' cried she. 'Yes, miss,' said I, sheepishly, 'but we can't always have what we like you see; I ought to have held my shilling tighter.'

'Your shilling,' cries she. 'Oh!' and she dashed her hand into her pocket and took out her purse, and I could see her beautiful white fingers tremble with eagerness as they dived among the coin. She soon bought the loaf, and, as she handed it to me, I happened to look in her face and her cheek was red and her eyes quite brimming: her quick woman's heart had told her the truth, that it was a well-dressed and tolerably well-behaved man's last shilling, and he returning after years of travel to his native land.

I am sure, until the young lady felt for me, I thought nothing of it; I had been at my last shilling more than once. But when I saw she thought it hard, I began to think it was hard, and I remember the water came into my own eyes. Heaven bless her, and may she never want a shilling in her pocket, nor a kind heart near her to show her the world is not all made of stone.

We had no money to pay our passage, and we found Mr. Yates somewhat embarrassed; we had cost him a thousand or two and no return. So, whilst he wrote to Mons. Huguet, that came to pass in England which we had always just contrived to stave off abroad.

The elephant was pawned.

And now I became of use to the proprietors I arranged with the mortgagees, and they made the spout a show-place. I used to exhibit her and her tricks, and with the proceeds I fed her, and Elliot, and myself.

We had been three weeks in pledge, when, one fine morning, as I was showing off seated on the elephant's back, I heard a French exclamation of surprise and joy; I looked down and there was M. Huguet. I came down to him, and he, whose quick eye saw a way through me out of drunken Elliot, gave a loose to his feelings and embraced me à la Française: 'which made the common people very much to admire' as the song has it, also a polite howl of derision greeted our continental affection. M. Huguet put his hand into his pocket, and we got out of limbo, and were let loose upon suffering humanity once more.

They talk as if English gold did every-thing; but it was French gold bought us off, I know that; for I saw it come out of his pocket.

As soon as we were redeemed, we took an engagement at Astley's, and, during this en-gagement, cadaverous Tom, finding we could master her, used to attend less and less to her, and more and more to brandy

A certain baker who brought her loaves every morning for breakfast, used to ask me to let him feed her himself. He admired her, and took this way of making her fond of him. One day I had left these two friends and their loaves together for a minute, when I heard a fearful cry. I knew the sound too well by this time and, as I ran back, I had the sense to hallo at her; this saved the man's life: at the sound of my voice she dropped him from a height of about twelve feet, and he rolled away like a ball of worsted. I dashed in, up with the pitchfork and into her like lightning, and, while the blood was squirting out of her from a hundred little prongholes, the poor baker limped away

Any gentleman or lady who wishes to know how a man feels when seized by an elephant, preparatory to being squelched, can consult this person; he is a respectable tradesman; his name is Johns: he lives near Astley's Theatre, or used to, and for obvious reasons can tell you this one anecdote out of many such better than I can; that is if he has not forgotten it, and *I dare say he hasn't*—ask him!

After Astley's, Drury Lane engaged us to play second to the Lions of Mysore; rather a down-come; but we went. In this theatre we behaved wonderfully Notwithstanding the number of people continually buzzing about us, we kept our temper and did not smash a single one of these human gnats so trying to our little female irritability and feeble nerves. The only thing we did wrong was we broke through a granite mountain and fell down on to the plains, and hurt our knee, and broke one super,—only one.

The Lions of Mysore went a starring to Liverpool, and we accompanied them. Whilst we were there the cholera broke out in England, and M. Huguet summoned us hastily to France. We brushed our hats, put on our gloves and walked at one stretch from Liverpool to Dover. There we embarked for Boulogne; Djek, cadaverous Tom, wolf-skin-lamb Pippin, and myself. I was now in Huguet's service at fifty francs a week, as coadjutor and successor of cadaverous Tom, whose demise was hourly expected even by us who were hardened by use to his appearance, which was that of the ghost of delirium tremens. We arrived off Boulogne Pier; but there we were boarded by men in uniforms and moustaches, and questions put about the cholera, which disease the civic authorities of Boulogne were determined to keep on the other side of the channel. The captain's answer proving satisfactory, we were allowed to run into the port.

In landing anywhere Djek and her attendants had always to wait till the other passengers had got clear, and we did so on this occasion. At length our turn came; but we had no sooner crossed the gangway, and touched French ground, than a movement took place on the quay, and a lot of bayonets bristled in our faces, and ' halte là ' was the word. We begged an explanation; in answer an officer glared with eyes like saucers and pointed with his finger at Elliot. The truth flashed on us. The Frenchmen were afraid of cholera coming over from England, and here was a man who looked plague cholera or death himself in person. We remonstrated through an interpreter, but Tom's face was not to be refuted by words. Some were for sending us back home to so diseased a country as this article must have come out of; but milder measures prevailed. They set apart for our use a little corner of the quay, and there they roped us in and sentinelled us. And so for four days, in the polished kingdom of France, we dwelt in a hut ruder far than any on the banks of the Ohio. Drink for ever! At last as Tom Coffin got neither a worse nor a better colour, they listened to reason and let us loose upon the nation at large, and away we tramped for Paris.

Times were changed with us in one respect; we no longer marched to certain victory; our long ill-success in America had lessened our arrogance, and we crept along towards Paris. But luckily for us we had now a presiding head and a good one. The soul of business is puffing; and no man puffed better than our chief M. Huguet. Half way between Boulogne and Paris we were met by a cavalier carrying our instructions how we were to enter Paris; and, arrived at St. Denis, instead of going straight on, we skirted the town, and made our formal entry by the Bois de Boulogne and the Arch of Triumph. Huguet had come to terms with Franconi, and, to give Djek's engagement more public importance, Franconi's whole troop were ordered out to meet us and escort us in. They paraded up and down the Champs Elysées first, to excite attention and inquiry, and, when the public were fairly agog, our cavalcade formed outside the barrier and came glittering and prancing through the arch. An elephant has her ups and her downs like the rest. Djek, the despised of Kentucky and Virginia, burst on Paris, the centre of a shining throng. Franconi's bright amazons and exquisite cavaliers rode to and fro our line carrying sham messages with earnest faces; Djek was bedecked with ribbons and seemed to tread more majestically, and our own hearts beat higher, as, amidst grace and beauty, and pomp, sun shining—hats waving—feathers bending—mob cheering—trumpets crowing— and flints striking fire, we strode proudly into the great city, the capital of pleasure.

CHAPTER X.

——•——

THESE were bright days to me. I was set over old Tom—fancy that; and my salary doubled his: I had fifty francs a week, and cleared as much more by showing her privately in her stable.

Money melts in London; it evaporates in Paris. Pippin was a great ‹favourite both with men and women behind the scenes at Franconi's: he introduced me to charming companions of both sexes; gaiety reigned, and tin and morals ‘made themselves air, into which they vanished,’ Shakspere.

Towards the close of her engagement Djek

made one of her mistakes; she up with her rightful heir and broke his ribs against the side scenes.

We nearly had to stop her performances! we could not mend our rightful heir by next night, and substitutes did not pour in. 'I won't go on with her,' 'I won't play with her,' was a cry that even the humblest and neediest began to raise. I am happy to say that she was not under my superintendence when this rightful heir came to grief.

And now the cholera came to Paris, and theatricals of all sorts declined, for there was a real tragedy playing in every street. The deaths were very numerous and awfully sudden; people were struck down in the streets as if by lightning; gloom and terror hung over all.

When this terrible disease is better known it will be found to be of the nature of strong poison, and its cure, if any, will be strychnine, belladonna, or likelier still some quick and

deadly mineral poison that kills the healthy
with cramps and discoloration.

In its rapid form cholera is not to be told
from quick poison, and hence sprung up among
the lower order in Paris a notion that wholesale poisoning was on foot.

Pippin and I were standing at the door of
a wine-shop waiting for our change; his wild
appearance attracted first one and then
another: little knots of people collected and
eyed us: then they began to talk and murmur
and cast suspicious glances. 'Come away,' said
Pippin rather hastily. We walked off—they
walked after us increasing like a snowball, and
they murmured louder and louder. I asked
Pippin what the fools were gabbling about;
he told me they suspected us of being the
poisoners; at this I turned round and being
five feet four, and English, was for punching
some of their heads; but the athletic pacific
Italian would not hear of it, much less co-
operate and now they surrounded us just at

the corner of one of the bridges, lashing themselves into a fury, and looking first at us, and
then at the river below. Pippin was as
white as death, and I thought it was all up
myself, when by good luck a troop of mounted
gendarmes issued from the palace. Pippin
hailed them; they came up, and, after hearing
both sides, took us under their protection, and
off we marched between two files of cavalry,
followed by the curses of a superficial populace.
Extremes don't do. Pippin was the colour of
ink, Elliot of paper: both their mugs fell
under suspicion and nearly brought us to
grief.

Franconi closed, and Djek Huguet and Co.
started on a provincial tour.

They associated themselves on this occasion
with Michelet, who had some small wild
animals, such as lions, tigers, and leopards.

Our first move was to Versailles. Here we
built a show-place and exhibited Djek, not as
an actress, but as a private elephant, in which

capacity she did the usual elephant business, besides a trick or two that most of them have not brains enough for; whereof anon.

Michelet was the predecessor of Van Amburgh and Carter, and did everything they do a dozen years before they were ever heard of; used to go into the lions' den, pull them about, and put his head down their throats and their paws round his neck, &c. &c.

I observed this man and learned something from him. Besides that general quickness and decision, which is necessary with wild animals, I noticed that he was always on the look out for mischief, and always punished it before it came. Another point, he always attacked the offending part, and so met the evil in front; for instance, if one of his darlings curled a lip and showed a tooth, he hit him over the mouth that moment and no-where else; if one elongated a claw he hit him over the foot like lightning. He read the whole crew as I had learned to read Djek, and conquered their malice by means of that marvellous cowardice which they all show if they can see no sign of it in you.

There are no two ways with wild beasts. If there is a single white spot in your heart—leave them; for your life will be in danger every moment. If you can despise them, and keep the rod always in sight, they are your humble servants; nobody more so.

Our exhibition, successful at first, began to flag; so then the fertile brain of M. Huguet had to work. He proposed to his partner to stand a tiger and he would stand a bull, and 'we will have a joint-stock fight like the King of Oude.' Michelet had his misgivings; but Huguet overruled him. That ingenious gentleman then printed bills advertising for a certain day a fight between a real Bengal tiger and a ferocious bull that had just gored a man to death. This done, he sent me round the villages to find and hire a bull; 'mind you get a mild one, or I shall have to pay for

JACK OF ALL TRADES.

a hole in the tiger's leather.' I found one
which the owner consented to risk for so much
money down, and the damage he should sustain
from tiger to be valued independently by two
farmers after the battle.

The morning of the fight Pippin and I went
for our bull, and took him out of the yard
towards Versailles; but when we had gone
about two hundred yards, he became uneasy,
looked round, sniffed about and finally turned
round spite of all our efforts, and paced home
again. We remonstrated with the proprietor.
' Oh,' said he. ' I forgot—he won't start without
the wench.' So the wench in question was sent
for (his companion upon amatory excursions)
she went with us and launched us towards
Versailles. This done, she returned home, and
we marched on; but before we had gone
a furlong, Taurus showed symptoms of uneasiness; these increased, and at last he
turned round and walked tranquilly home.
We hung upon him, thrashed him and bullied

P

him all to no purpose. His countenance was placid but his soul resolved, and—he walked home slowly, but inevitably so then there was nothing for it but to let him have the wench all the way to the tiger; and she would not go to Versailles till she had put on some new finery, short waist, coal-scuttle bonnet &c. More time lost with that—and, when we did arrive in the arena, the spectators were tired of waiting. The bull stood in the middle confused and stupid. The tiger was in his cage in a corner; we gave him time to observe his prey and then we opened the door of his cage.

A shiver ran through the audience; (they were all seated in boxes looking down on the area).

A moment more and the furious animal would spring upon his victim and his fangs and claws sink deep into its neck &c. &c. vide book of travels.

One moment succeeded to another and

nothing occurred. The ferocious animal lay quiet in his cage, and showed no sign; so then we poked the ferocious animal—he snarled but would not venture out. When this had lasted a long time, the spectators began to doubt his ferocity, and to goose the ferocious animal. So I got a red hot iron and nagged him behind. He gave a yell of dismay and went into the arena like a shot. He took no notice of the bull: all he thought of was escape from the horrors that surrounded him; winged by terror he gave a tremendous spring and landed his fore-paws on the boxes, stuck fast and glared in at the spectators. They rushed out yelling. He dug his hind-claws into the wood-work and by slow and painful degrees clambered into the boxes. When he got in, the young and active were gone home, and he ran down the stairs among the old people that could not get clear so quick as the rest. He was so frightened at the people that he skulked and hid himself in a corn-field, and the people were so frightened at him that they ran home and locked their street-doors. So one coward made many.

They thought the poor wretch had *attacked* them, and the journal next day maintained this view of the transaction, and the town to this day believes it. We netted our striped coward with four shutters, and kicked him into his cage.

The bull went home with 'the wench,' and to this day his thick skull has never comprehended what the deuce he went to Versailles for.

This was how we competed with oriental monarchs.

We marched southward, through Orleans, Tours &c. to Bordeaux, and were pretty well received in all these places except at one small place whose name I forget. Here they hissed her out of the town at sight. It turned out she had been there before and pulverized a brush-maker, a popular man amongst them.

Soon after Bordeaux she had words with the lions; they, in their infernal conceit, thought themselves more attractive than Djek. It is vice versa, and by a long chalk said Djek and Co. The parties growled a bit, then parted to meet no more in this world.

From Bordeaux we returned by another route to Paris; for we were only starring it in the interval of our engagement as an actress with Franconi. We started one morning from —— with light hearts, our faces turned towards the gay city; Elliot, Pippin and I. Elliot and I walked by the side of the elephant, Pippin walking some forty yards in the rear. He never trusted himself nearer to her on a march.

We were plodding along in this order, when, all in a moment, without reason or warning of any sort, she spun round between us on one heel like a thing turning on a

pivot, and strode back like lightning at
Pippin.   He screamed and ran, but before
he could take a dozen steps, she was upon
him and struck him down with her trunk and
trampled upon him, she then wheeled round
and trudged back as if she had merely stopped
to brush off a fly, or pick up a stone.   After
the first moment of stupefaction both Elliot
and I had run after her with all the speed we
had: but so rapid was her movement, and so
instantaneous the work of death, that we only
met her on her return from her victim.   I
will not shock the reader by describing the
state in which we found our poor comrade:
but he was crushed to death: he never spoke,
and I believe and trust he never felt anything
for the few minutes that breath lingered in
his body   We kneeled down and raised him
and spoke to him but he could not hear us.
When Djek got her will of one of us, all our
hope used to be to see the man die; and so
it was with poor dear Pippin; mangled, and

life impossible, we kneeled down and prayed to God for his death; and by Heaven's mercy, I think in about four minutes from the time he got his death-blow, his spirit passed away, and our well-beloved comrade and friend was nothing now but a lump of clay on our hands.

We were some miles from any town or village, and did not know what to do, and how to take him to a resting-place; at last we were obliged to tie the body across the proboscis, and cover it as well as we could, and so we made his murderess carry him to the little town of La Palice; yes, La Palice. Here we stopped, and a sort of inquest was held, and M. Huguet attended and told the old story; said the man had been cruel to her and she had put up with it as long as she could. Verdict—'Served him right,'—and so we lied over our poor friend's murdered body, and buried him with many sighs in the little churchyard of La Palice, and then trudged on sad and downcast towards the gay capital.

CHAPTER XI.

I THINK a lesson is to be learned from this sad story. Too much fear is not prudence. Had poor Pippin walked with Elliot and me alongside the elephant, she dared not have attacked him. But through fear he kept forty yards in the rear, and she saw a chance to get him by himself; and, from my knowledge of her, I have little doubt she had meditated this attempt for months before she carried it out. Poor Pippin!

We arrived in Paris to play with Franconi. Now it happened to be inconvenient to Franconi to fulfil his engagement. He accordingly declined us. M. Huguet was angry: threatened legal proceedings. Franconi answered, 'Where is Pippin?' Huguet shut up. Then Franconi followed suit; if hard pressed, he threatened to declare in open court that it was out of humanity alone he declined to fulfil his engagement. This stopped M. Huguet's mouth altogether. He took a place on the Boulevard, and we showed her and her tricks at three prices, and did a rattling business. Before we had been a fortnight in Paris old Tom Elliot died at the Hospital Dubois, and I became her vizier at a salary of one hundred francs per week.

Having now the sole responsibility, I watched her as you would a powder-magazine lighted by gas. I let nobody but M. Huguet go near her in my absence. This gentleman continued to keep her sweet on him with lumps of sugar, and to act as her showman when she exhibited publicly.

One day we had a message from the

Tuileries, and we got the place extra clean;
and the king's children paid her a visit—a
lot of little chaps — I did not know their
names, but I suppose it was Prince Joinville,
Aumale and cetera.   All I know is that while
these little Louis Philippes were coaxing her,
and feeding her, and cutting about her and
sliding down her, and I was a telling them
she was a duck, the perspiration was running
down my back one moment and cold shivers
the next, and I thanked Heaven devoutly
when the young gents went back to their
papa and mamma and no bones broken.   The
young gentlemen reported her affability, and
my lies, to the king, and he engaged her to
perform gratis in the Champs Elysées during
the three days' fête.   Fifteen hundred francs
for this.

But Huguet was penny wise and pound
foolish to agree: for it took her gloss off.
Showed her gratis to half the city.

Among Djek's visitors came one day a

pretty young lady, a nursery-governess to
some nobleman's children, whose name I
forget, but he was English. The children
were highly amused with Djek, and quite
loath to go. The young lady, who had a
smattering of English as I had of French,
put several questions to me. I answered
them more polite than usual on account of
her being pretty, and I used a privilege I
had and gave her an order for free admission
some other day. She came, with only one
child, which luckily was one of those deeply
meditative ones that occur but rarely, and
only bring out a word every half-hour; so
mademoiselle and I had a chat, which I found
so agreeable that I rather neglected the
general public for her. I made it my business to learn where she aired the children,
and, one vacant morning, dressed in the top
of the fashion, I stood before her in the garden of the Tuileries; she gave a half-start
and a blush, and seemed very much struck

with astonishment at this rencontre : she was a little less astonished next week when the same thing happened, but still she thought these coincidences remarkable, and said so. In short I paid my addresses to Mademoiselle ——. She was a charming brunette from Geneva, greatly my superior in education and station. I was perfectly conscious of this, and instantly made this calculation 'all the better for me if I can win her.' But the reader knows my character by this time, and must have observed how large a portion of it effrontery forms. I wrote to her every day, sometimes in the French language; no not in the French language ; in French words. She sometimes answered in English words : she was very pretty and very interesting, and I fancied her. When a man is in love he can hardly see difficulties : I pressed her to marry me, and I believed she would consent. When I came to this point the young lady's gaiety declined, and when I was painting her pictures of our conjugal happiness, she used to sigh instead of brightening at the picture : at last I pressed her so hard that she consented to write to Geneva, and ask her parents' consent to our union : when the letter went I was in towering spirits : I was now in the zenith of my prosperity : the risks I had run with Djek were rewarded by a heavy salary and the post of honour near her, and, now that I was a little weary of roaming the world alone with an elephant, fate had thrown in my way a charming companion who would cheer the weary road.

Dreams.

The old people at Geneva saw my position with another eye. 'He is a servant liable to lose his place at any moment by any one of a hundred accidents, and his profession is a discreditable one : why he is a showman.'

They told her all this in language so plain that she would never show me the letter. I was for defying their advice and authority, but she would not hear of it. I was forced to temporise. 'In a month's time' said I to myself 'her scruples will melt away.' But in less than a fortnight the order came for us to march into Flanders. I communicated this cruel order to my sweetheart; she turned pale and made no secret of her attachment to me and of the pain she felt at parting. Every evening before we left Paris I saw her and implored her to trust herself to me and leave Paris as my wife. She used to smile at my pictures of wedded happiness, and cry the next minute because she dared not give herself and me that happiness; but with all this she was firm, and would not fly in her parents' face.

At last came a sad and bitter hour: hat in hand, as the saying is, I made a last desperate endeavour to persuade her to be mine, and not to let this parting take place at all. She was much agitated, but firm; and, the more I said, the firmer she became. So at last I grew frantic and reproached her. I called her a cold-hearted coquette, and we parted in anger and despair.

Away into the wide world again, not, as I used to start on these pilgrimages, with a stout heart and iron nerves, but cold and weary and worn out before the journey had begun. As we left Paris behind us I had but one feeling, that the best of life was at an end for me. My limbs took me along like machinery, but my heart was a lump of ice inside me, and I would have thanked any man for knocking me on the head and ending the monotonous farce of my existence: ay gentlefolks, even a poor mechanic can feel like this when the desire of his heart is baulked for ever.

Trudge! trudge! trudge! for ever and ever.

Tramp! tramp! tramp! for ever and ever.

A man gets faint and weary of it at last,

and there comes a time when he pines for a hearth-stone, and a voice he can believe, a part at least of what it says, and a Sunday of some sort now and then; and my time was come to long for these things, and for a pretty and honest face about me to stand for the one bit of peace, and the one bit of truth, in my vagabond-charlatan life.

I lost my appetite and sleep, and was very nearly losing heart altogether. My clothes hung about me like bags—I got so thin. It was my infernal occupation that cured me after all. Djek gave me no time even for despair: the moment I became her sole guardian I had sworn on my knees she should never kill another man; judge whether I had to look sharp after her to keep the biped from perjury and the quadruped from murder. I slept with her—rose early—fed her—walked twenty miles with her, or exhibited her all day, sometimes did both, and at night rolled into the straw beside her too deadly tired to feel all my unhappiness; and so, after awhile, time and toil blunted my sense of disappointment, and I trudged and tramped and praised Djek's moral qualities in the old routine. Only now and then when I saw the country lads in France or Belgium going to church dressed in their best with their sweethearts, and I in prison in the stable with my four-legged hussey, waiting perhaps till dark to steal out and march to some fresh town, I used to feel as heavy as lead, and as bitter as wormwood, and wish we were all dead together by way of a change.

A man needs a stout heart to go through the world at all: but most of all he needs it for a roving life; don't you believe any other, no matter who tells you.

With this brief notice of my feelings I pass over two months' travel. All through, I spare the reader much, though I dare say he doesn't see it.

Sir the very names of the places I have

visited would fill an old-fashioned map of Europe.

Talk of Ulysses and his travels; he never saw the tenth part of what I have gone through.

I have walked with Djek farther than round the world during the eleven years I trudged beside her: it is only 24,000 miles round the world.

After a year's pilgrimage we found ourselves at Doncheray near Sedan.

Here we had an incident. Mons. Huguet was showing her to the public with the air of a prince and in his maréchal of France costume, glittering with his theatrical cross of the legion of honour. He was not particular what he put on so that it shone, and looked well. He sent me for something connected with the performance, a pistol I think. I had hardly ten steps to go, but during the time I was out of her sight, I heard a man cry out and the elephant snort. I ran back

halloing as I came. As I ran in I found the
elephant feeling for something in the straw
with her foot, and the people rushing out of
the doors in dismay; the moment she saw me
she affected innocence, but trembled from head
to foot. I drew out from the straw a thing
you would have taken for a scarecrow, or a
bundle of rags. It was my master, M. Huguet,
his glossy hat battered, his glossy coat stained
and torn, and his arm broken in two places;
a moment more and her foot would have been
on him and his soul crushed out of his body.

The people were surprised when they saw
the furious snorting monster creep into a
corner to escape a little fellow five feet four,
who got to the old weapon, pitchfork, and
drove it into every part of her but her head.
She hid that in the corner the moment she
saw blood in my eye.

We got poor M. Huguet to bed, and a
doctor from the hospital to him, and a
sorrowful time he had of it; and so after

standing good for twelve years, lump sugar fell to the ground.   Pitchfork held good.

At night more than a hundred people came to see whether I was really so hardy as to sleep with this ferocious animal. To show them my sense of her I lay down between her legs.   On this she lifted her fore-feet singly and with the utmost care and delicacy drew them back over my body.

As soon as M. Huguet's arm was set, and doing well, he followed us—(we had got into France by this time), and came in along with the public to admire us, and, to learn how the elephant stood affected towards him now, he cried out in his most ingratiating way—in sugared tones—'Djek my boy, Djek.'   At this sound Djek raised a roar of the most infernal rage, and Huguet, who knew her real character well enough, though he pretended not to, comprehended that her heart was now set upon his extinction, malgré twelve years of lump sugar.

He sent for me, and with many expressions of friendship offered me the invaluable animal for thirty thousand francs. I declined her without thanks. 'Then I shall have *the pleasure* of killing her to-morrow' said the Frenchman, 'and what will become of your salary mon pauvre garçon?'

In short he had me in a fix and used his power. I bought her of him for 20,000 francs, to be paid by instalments. I gave him the first instalment, a five-franc piece, and walked out of the wine-shop her sole proprietor.

The sense of property is pleasant even when we have not paid for the article.

That night I formed my plans; there was no time to lose, because I had only a thousand francs in the world and she ate a thousand francs a week or nearly. I determined to try Germany, a poor country, but one which being quite inland could not have become callous to an elephant, perhaps had never seen

one. I shall never forget the fine clear
morning I started on my own account. The
sun was just rising, the birds were tuning
and all manner of sweet smells came from the
fields and the hedges. Djek seemed to step
out more majestically than when she was
another man's : my heart beat high. Eleven
years ago I had started the meanest of her
slaves, I had worked slowly, painfully but
steadily up, and now I was actually her lord
and master, and half the world before me with
the sun shining on it.

The first town I showed her at as mine was
Verdun, and the next day I wrote to Mademoiselle —— at Paris to tell her of the change
in my fortunes. This was the only letter I had
sent ; for we parted bad friends. I received a
kinder answer than the abrupt tone of my
letter deserved. She congratulated me and
thanked me for remembering that whatever
good fortune befel me must give her particular
pleasure, and in the postscript she told me she

was just about to leave Paris and return to her parents in Switzerland.

Djek crossed into Prussia, tramped that country and penetrated into the heart of Germany. As I had hoped, she descended on this nation with all the charm of novelty, and used to clear the copper* out of a whole village. I remember early in this trip being at a country inn. I saw rustics male and female dressed in their Sunday clothes coming over the hills from every side to one point. I thought there must be a fair or something. I asked the landlord what they were all coming for: he said, ' Why you to be sure.' They never saw such a thing in their lives and never will again.

In fact at one or two small places we were stopped by the authorities, who had heard that we carried more specie out of little towns than the circulating medium would bear.

---

* Germany is mostly made of copper. A bucket-full of farthings was a common thing for me to have in my carriage.

In short my first coup was successful.
After six months' Germany, Bavaria, Prussia
&c., I returned to the Rhine at Strasbourg
with eight thousand francs. During all this
time she never hurt a soul, I watched her so
fearfully close. So being debarred from murder
she tried arson.

At a place in Bavaria her shed was suddenly
observed to be in flames, and we saved her
with difficulty.

The cause never transpired until now;
but I saw directly how it had been done: I
had unwarily left my coat in her way. The
pockets were found emptied of all their
contents, amongst which was a lucifer-box,
fragments of which I found amongst the
straw. She had played with this in her
trunk, hammering it backwards and forwards
against her knee, dropping the lighted matches
into the straw when they stung her, and very
nearly roasted her own beef the mischievous
uneasy devil.

My readers will not travel with an elephant, but business of some sort will fall to the lot of them soon or late, and as charlatanry is the very soul of modern business it may not be amiss to show how the humble artisan worked his elephant.

We never allowed ourselves to drop casually upon any place like a shower of rain.

A man in bright livery green and gold mounted on a showy horse used to ride into the town or village, and go round to all the inns making loud inquiries about their means of accommodation for the elephant and her train. Four hours after him, the people being now a little agog, another green and gold man came in on a trained horse, and inquired for No. 1: as soon as he had found him, the two rode together round the town — No. 2 blowing a trumpet and proclaiming the elephant; the nations she had instructed in the wonders of nature; the kings she had amused; her grandeur, her intelligence, and above all her dove-like disposition.

This was allowed to ferment for some hours, and, when expectation was at its height, the rest of the cavalcade used to heave in sight—Djek bringing up the rear. Arrived I used to shut her in out of sight, and send all my men and horses round, parading, trumpeting and pasting bills; so that at last the people were quite ripe for her, and then we went to work: and thus the humble artisan and his elephant cut a greater dash than lions and tigers and mountebanks and quacks, and drew more money.

Here is one of my programmes: only I must remark that I picked up my French, where I picked up the sincerity it embodies, in the circuses, coulisses, and cabarets of French towns so that I can patter French as fast as you like; but of course I know no more about it than a pig—not to really know it.

Par permission de M. le Maire

Le grand

ELEPHANT

du Roi de Siam

Du Cirque Olympique Franconi.

Mlle. Djek,

Eléphant colossal, de onze pieds de hauteur et du poids de neuf mille liv., est le plus grand éléphant que l'on ait vu en Europe.

M. H. B. Lott, naturaliste, pourvoyeur des ménageries des diverses cours d'Europe, actionnaire du Cirque Olympique et propriétaire de ce magnifique éléphant, qu'il a dressé au point de le présenter au public dans une pièce théâtrale qui fut créée pour Madlle. Djek il y a trois ans et demi, et qui a eu un si grand succès, sous le nom de l'Eléphant du Roi de Siam.

Le propriétaire, dans son voyage autour du monde, eut occasion d'acheter cet énorme quadrupède, qui le prit en affection, et qui, depuis onze ans qu'il le possède, ne s'est jamais dementi, se plaît à écouter son maître et exécute avec punctualité tout ce qu'il lui indique de faire.

Mlle. Djek, qui est dans toute la force de sa taille, a maintenant cent vingt-cinq ans ; elle a onze pieds de hauteur—et pèse neuf mille livres.

Sa consommation dans les vingt-quatre heures excède deux cent livres—quarante livres de pain pour son déjeûner : à midi, du son et de l'avoine ; le soir, des pommes-de-terre ou du riz cuit ; et la nuit du foin et de la paille.

C'est le même éléphant qui a combattu la lionne de M. Martin. Cette lionne en furie, qu'une imprudence fit sortir de sa cage, s'élance sur M. H. B. Lott qui se trouvait auprès de son éléphant ; voyant le danger il se réfugie derrière une des jambes de ce bon animal, qui relève sa trompe pour le protéger.* La lionne allait saisir M. H. B. Lott; l'éléphant la voit, rabat sa trompe, l'enveloppe, l'étouffe, la jette at loin, et l'aurait écrasée, si son maître ne lui eut dit de ne pas continuer.

Elle a ensuite allongé sa trompe, frappé du pied, criant et témoignant la satisfaction, qu'elle éprouvait d'avoir sauvé son ami d'une mort certaine, comme on a pu voir dans les journaux en février 1832.

Dans les cours des séances, on lui fera faire tous ses grands exercices qui sont dignes d'admiration, dont le grand nombre ne permet pas d'en donner l'analyse dans cette affiche, et qu'il faut voir pour l'en faire une idée juste.

Prix d'entrée : Premières   Secondes
—Les militaires et les infants, moitié.

---

* I am a dull fellow now, as you see. But you must allow I have been a man of imagination.

I don't think but what my countrymen will understand every word of the above, but as there are a great number of Frenchmen in London who will read this, I think it would look unkind not to translate it into English for their benefit.

By permission of the Worshipful the Mayor

the great

ELEPHANT

of the King of Siam

from Franconi's Olympic Circus.

Mademoiselle Djek

Colossal Elephant, eleven feet high and weighs nine thousand pounds. The largest Elephant ever seen in Europe.

Mr. H. B. Lott, naturalist, who supplies the menageries of the various courts of Europe, shareholder in the Olympic Circus, and proprietor of this magnificent elephant, which he has trained to such a height that he will present her to the public in a dramatic piece which was written for her three years and a half ago and had a great success under the title of the Elephant of the King of Siam.*

The proprietor, in his voyage round the globe, was fortunate enough to purchase this enormous quadruped, which became attached to him, and has been eleven years in his possession, during which time she has never once forgotten herself and executes with obedient zeal whatever he bids her.

Mdlle. Djek has now arrived at her full growth being one hundred and twenty-five years of age: she is eleven feet high and weighs nine thousand pounds. Her daily consumption exceeds two hundred pounds: she

* My literary gent and me we nearly had words over this bit. 'Why it is all nominative case,' says he. 'Well' says I 'you can't have too much of a good thing. Can you better it?' says I. 'Better it' says he, 'why I could not have come within a mile of it;' and he grinned: so I shut him up—for once.

takes forty pounds of bread for her breakfast, at noon barley and oats, in the evening potatoes or rice cooked, and at night hay and straw

This is the same elephant that fought with Mr. Martin's lioness. The lioness, whom the carelessness of the attendants allowed to escape from her cage, dashed furiously at Mr. H. B. Lott; fortunately he was near his elephant, and seeing the danger took refuge behind one of the legs of that valuable animal; she raised her trunk in her master's defence. The lioness made to seize him : but the elephant lowered her trunk, seized the lioness, choked her, flung her to a distance and would have crushed her to death if Mr. Lott had not commanded her to desist. After that she extended her trunk, stamped with her foot, trumpeting and showing her satisfaction, at having saved her friend from certain death; full accounts of which are to be seen in the journals of February 1832.

In the course of the exhibition she will go through all her exercises, which are wonderful, and so numerous that it is impossible to enumerate them in this bill : they must be seen to form a just idea of them.

Prices : First places   Second Soldiers and children half-price.

Djek and I used to make our bow to our audiences in the following fashion. I came on with her and said 'Otez mon chapeau pour saluer:' then she used to take off my hat, wave it gracefully and replace it on my head—she then proceeded to pick up twenty five-franc pieces one after another and keep them piled in the extremity of her trunk. She also fired pistols, and swept her den with a broom in a most painstaking and ludicrous way.

But perhaps her best business in a real judge's eye was drinking a bottle of wine. The reader will better estimate this feat if he will fancy himself an elephant and lay down

R

the book now and ask himself how he would
do it——and read the following afterwards.

The bottle (cork drawn) stood before her.
She placed the finger and thumb of her proboscis on the mouth, made a vacuum by suc-
tion, and then, suddenly inverting the bottle,
she received the contents in her trunk ; the
difficulty now was to hold the bottle, which
she would not have broken for a thousand
pounds (my lady thought less of killing ten
men than breaking a saucer) and yet not let
the liquor run from her flesh-pipe. She rapidly
shifted her hold to the centre of the bottle
and worked it by means of the wrinkles in
her proboscis to the bend of it. Then she
griped it and at the same time curled round
her trunk into a sloping position and let the
wine run down her throat. This done, she
resumed the first position of her trunk, and
worked the bottle back towards her finger,
suddenly snapped hold of it by the neck and
handed it gracefully to me.

With this exception it was not her public
tricks that astonished me most. The principle of all these tricks is one. An animal is
taught to lay hold of things at command, and
to shift them from one place to another. You
vary the thing to be laid hold of, but the act
is the same. In her drama, which was so
effective on the stage, Djek did nothing out
of the way. She merely went through certain mechanical acts at a word of command
from her keeper, who was unseen or unnoticed
i. e. he was either at the wing in his fustian
jacket, or on the stage with her in gimcrack
and gold as one of a lot of slaves or courtiers
or what not. Between ourselves, a single
trick I have several times caught her doing
on her own account proved more for her intelligence than all these. She used to put
her eye to a keyhole. Ay that she would,
and so watch for hours to see what devil's
trick she could do with impunity—she would
see me out of the way and then go to work.

Where there was no keyhole I have seen her pick the knot out of a deal-board, and squint through the little hole she had thus made.

A dog comes next to an elephant: but he is not up to looking through a keyhole, or a crack. He can think of nothing better than snuffing under the door.

At one place, being under a granary, she worked a hole in the ceiling no bigger than a thimble, and sucked down sacksful of grain before she was found out. Talk of the half-reasoning elephant: she seldom met a man that could match her in reasoning—to a bad end. Her weak points were her cruelty and cowardice, and by this latter Tom Elliot and I governed her with a rod of iron— vulgarly called a pitchfork. If a mouse pottered about the floor in her stable Djek used to tremble all over, and whine with terror till the little monster was gone. A ton shaken by an ounce.

I have seen her start back in dismay from

a small feather floating in the air. If her heart had been as stout as her will to do mischief was strong, mankind must have risen to put her down.

Almost all you have ever heard about the full grown elephant's character is a pack of falsities. They are your servants by fear, or they are your masters. Two years ago an elephant killed his keeper at Liverpool or Manchester I forget which. Out came the "Times:" he had pronged him six weeks before; how well I knew the old lie; it seldom varies a syllable. That man died not because he had pronged the animal but because he hadn't, or not enough.

Spare the pitchfork—spoil the elephant.

There is another animal people misconstrue just as bad.

The hyena.

Terrible fierce animal the hyena says Buffon and Co.; and the world echoes the chant.

Fierce; are they? you get a score of them

together in a yard, and you shall see me walk into the lot with nothing but a switch, and them try to get between the brick and the mortar with the funk, that is how fierce they are: and they are not only cowardly, but innocent, and affectionate into the bargain is the fierce hyena of Buffon and Co.: but indeed wild animals are sadly misunderstood: it is pitiable: and those that have the best character deserve it less than those that have the worst.

In one German town I met with something I should like to tell the sporting gents, for I don't think there is many that ever fell in with such a thing. But it is an old saying that what does happen has happened before, and may again, so I tell this to put them on their guard, especially in Germany. Well, it was a good town for business, and we staid several days: but before we had been there many hours my horses turned queer. Restless they were and uneasy. Sweated of their own accord. Stamped eternally. One in particular began to lose flesh. We examined the hay. It seemed particularly good, and the oats not amiss. Called the landlord in, and asked him if he could account for it. He stands looking at them; this one called Dick was all in a lather. 'Well I think I know now' said he; 'they are bewitched. You see there is an old woman in the next street that bewitches cattle, and she rides on your horses' backs all night you may take your oath.' Then he tells us a lot of stories, whose cow died after giving this old wench a rough word, and how she had been often seen to go across the meadows in the shape of a hare. 'She has a spite against me, the old sorceress,' says he. 'She has been at them; you had better send for the pastor.' 'Go for the farrier Jem' says I. So we had in the farrier. He sat on the bin and smoked his pipe in dead silence looking at them. 'They seem a little fidgetty' says he after about half an hour. So I turned *him* out of the stable. 'And I was in two minds about punching his head I was. Send for the veterinary surgeon No. 1.' He came. 'They have got some disorder' says he—'that is plain—nostrils are clear, too. Let me see them eat.' They took their food pretty well. Then he asked where we came from last. I told him. 'Well,' said he cheerfully 'this is a murrain I think. In this country we do invent a new murrain about every twenty years. We are about due now.' He spoke English this one, quite a fine gentleman. One of the grooms put in 'I think the water is poisoned.' 'Anyway' says another 'Dick will die if we stay here.' So then they both pressed me to leave the town. 'You know governor we can't afford to lose the horses.' Now I was clearing ten pounds a day in the place, and all expenses paid. So I looked blank. So did the veterinary. 'I wouldn't go,' says he, 'wait a day or two : then the disease will declare itself, and we shall know what we are doing.' You see gents he did not relish my taking a murrain out of his town, he was a veterinary. 'Whatever it is,' says he, 'you brought it with you.' 'Well now,' said I 'my opinion is I found it here. Did you notice anything at the last place, Nick?' 'No,' the grooms both bore me out. 'Oh!' says the vet. 'you can't go by that: it had not declared itself.' Well, if you will believe me (I often laugh when I think of it) it was not two minutes after he said that, that it did declare itself. It was Sunday morning, and Nick had got a clean shirt on: Nick was currying the very horse called Dick when all of a sudden the sleeve of his white shirt looked dirty. 'What now?' cries he, and comes to the light. 'I do believe it is vermin' says he, 'and if it is they are eaten up with it.' 'Vermin? what vermin can that be?' said I, 'have we invented a new vermin too?' They were no bigger than pins' points, looked like dust on his shirt. 'What do you say sir? is it vermin?' 'Not a doubt of it ' says the vet. ' These are poultry-lice, unless I am mistaken. Have you any hens anywhere near?' Both the grooms burst out, ' hens ? why there are full a hundred up in the hay-loft.' So that was the murrain: the hens had been tumbling in the hay the hay came down to the rack all alive with their vermin: and the vermin were eating the horses. We stopped that supply of hay; and what with currying and washing with a solut. the vet. gave us we cured that murrain—chicken-pox if any. We had a little scene at going away from this place. Landlord had agreed to charge nothing for the use of stabling we spent so much in other ways with him. In spite of that he put it down at the foot of the list. I would not pay. ' You must '—' I won't.' ' Then you shan't go till you do ; ' and with that he and his servants closed the great gates. The yard was entered by two great double doors like barn-doors, secured outside by a stout beam. So there he had us fast. It got wind and there was the whole population hooting outside, three thousand strong. Then it was 'come don't be a fool.'

'Don't you be a fool.'

'Stand clear,' said I to the man, 'we will alter our usual line of march this time, I'll take Djek from the rear to the front.' So they all formed behind me and Djek, two carriages, and six horses, all in order. 'Now' said I, 'landlord, you have had your joke : open the door, and let us part friends; we have been with you a week you know, and you have had one profit out of us, and another out of the townsfolk we brought to your bar—open the door.'

'Pay me my bill, and I'll open' says he. 'If I turned away one traveller from my stable for you I've turned away twenty.'

'A bargain is a bargain. Will you open? before she knocks your door into toothpicks.'

'Oh! I'll risk my door if you'll risk your beast. No! I won't open till I am paid.'

' Once, will you open ? '

' No.'

' Twice, will you open.—Thrice? '

'No.'

' Djek—Go ! '

She walked lazily at the door as if she did not see it. The moment she touched it, both doors were in the road, the beam was in half in the road; most times one thing stands, another goes : here it all went bodily on all sides like paper on a windy day, and the people went fastest of all. There was the yell of a multitude under our noses, then an empty street under our eyes. We marched on calm, majestical, and unruffled beneath the silent night.

Doors and bolts indeed—to a lady that had stepped through a brick wall before that day, an English brick wall.

CHAPTER XII.

FROM Strasbourg I determined to go into Switzerland : above all to Geneva—I could not help it; in due course of time and travel I arrived near Geneva and I sent forward my green and gold avant-couriers. But alas they returned with the doleful news that elephants were not admitted into that ancient city. The last elephant that had been there had done mischief, and, at the request of its proprietor Madlle. Garnier, a young lady whose conscience smote her, for she had had another elephant that killed one or two people in Venice, was publicly executed in the fortress.*

Fortunately (as I then thought) I had provided myself with testimonials from the mayor and governors of some score of towns through which we had passed. I produced these, and made friends in the town, particularly with a Dr. Mayo. At last we were admitted. Djek was proved a dove by such overpowering testimony. I had now paid M. Huguet six thousand francs and found myself possessed of five thousand more. Business was very good in Geneva. Djek very popular. Her intelligence and amiability became a by-word. I had but one bitter disappointment though. Madlle. —— never came to see us, and I was too sulky and too busy to hunt for her. Besides I said to myself ' All the world can find me, and if she cared a button for me she would come to light.' I tried to turn it off with the old song.

* They gave this elephant an ounce of prussic acid and an ounce of arsenic: neither of these sedatives producing any effect they fired a cannon ball through her neck.

' Now get ye gone ye scornful dame
If you are proud I'll be the same
I make no doubt that I shall find
As pretty a girl unto my mind.'

Behold me now at the climax of prosperity, dressed like a gentleman, driving a pair of horses, proprietor of a whole cavalcade and of an elephant, and, after clearing all expenses, making at the rate of full £600 per annum. There was a certain clergyman of the place used to visit us about every day and bring her cakes and things to eat, till he got quite fond of her, and believed that she returned his affection. I used to beg him not to go so close to her; on this his answer was, ' Why you say she is harmless as a chicken,' so then I had no more to say. Well, one unlucky day, I turned my back for a moment; before I could get back there were the old sounds, a snort of rage, and a cry of terror, and there was the poor minister in her trunk. At sight of me she dropped him, but two of his ribs were broken and he was quite insensible, and the people rushed out in terror. We raised the clergyman and carried him home, and in half an hour a mob was before the door and stones as big as your fists thrown in at the windows : this however was stopped by the authorities. But the next day my lady was arrested and walked off to the fortress and there confined. I remonstrated, expostulated —in vain. I had now to feed her and no return from her; ruin stared me in the face. So I went to law with the authorities. Law is slow, and Djek was eating all the time. Ruin looked nearer still. The law ate my green and gold servants and my horses, and still Djek remained in quod. Then I refused to feed her any longer; and her expenses fell upon the town. Her appetite and their poverty soon brought matters to a climax. They held a sort of municipal tribunal and tried her for an attempt at homicide. I got counsel to defend her, for I distrusted my own temper and French.

I can't remember half the fine things he said, but there was one piece of common sense I do remember, he said, 'The animal I believe is unconscious of her great strength and has committed a fatal error rather than a crime; still if you think she is liable to make such errors let her die rather than kill men. But how do you reconcile to your consciences to punish her proprietor, to rob him of his subsistence? *He* has committed no crime, *he* has been guilty of no want of caution. If therefore you take upon yourselves to punish the brute, be honest! buy her of the man first, and then assert your sublime office—destroy an animal that has offended morality But a city should be above wronging or robbing an individual.' When he sat down I thought my homicide was safe, for I knew Geneva could not afford to buy an elephant, without it was out of a Noah's ark.

But up gets an orator on the other side and attacked me; accused me of false representations, of calling a demon a duck. 'We have certain information from France, that this elephant has been always wounding and killing men up and down Europe these twenty years. Mons. Loett knew this by universal report and by being an eye-witness of more than one man's destruction '—here there was a sensation I can tell you. 'He has therefore forfeited all claims to consideration.' Then he thundered out 'Let no man claim to be wiser than Holy Writ; there we are told that a lie is a crime of the very deepest dye and here we see how for years falsehood has been murder.' Then I mind he took just the opposite line to my defender. Says he 'If I hesitate for a moment it is not for the man's sake, but for the brute's: but I do not hesitate. I could wish so majestic a creature might be spared for our instruction' says he 'that so wonderful a specimen of the Creator's skill might still walk the earth: but reason and justice and humanity say "No." There is an animal far smaller, yet ten times more important, for he has a soul; and this, the king of all the animals, is not safe while she lives: therefore she ought to die: weaker far than her in his individual strength, he is a thousand times stronger by combination and science—therefore she will die.'

When this infernal chatterbox shut up, my heart sunk into my shoes: he was a prig, but an eloquent one, and he walked into Djek and me till we were not worth half an hour's purchase.

For all that the council did not come to a decision on the spot, and I believe that if Djek had but been content to kill the laity as heretofore, we should have scraped through with a fine; but the fool must go and tear black cloth, and dig her own grave.

Two days after the trial, out came the sentence—Death!

With that modesty and good feeling which

belongs to most foreign governments they directed me to execute their sentence.

My answer came in English. 'I'll see you d—d and double d—d first, and then I won't.'

Meantime Huguet was persecuting poor heart-sick me for the remainder of her purchase-money, and, what with the delay, the expenses and the anxiety, I was so down and so at the end of my wits and my patience that her sentence fell on me like a blow on a chap that is benumbed, produced less effect upon me at the time than it does when I think of it now.

Well—curse them —one fine morning they ran a cannon up to the gate—loaded it—and bade me call the elephant, and bring her into a favourable position for being shot. I refused point blank in English as before. They threatened me for my contumacy. I answered they might shoot me if they liked, but I would not be the one to destroy my own livelihood.

So they had to watch their opportunity.

It was not long of coming.

She began to walk about, and presently the poor fool marched right up to the cannon's mouth and squinted down it. Then she turned and at last she crossed right before it. The gunner took the opportunity —applied his linstock and fired. There was a great tongue of flame and a cloud of smoke and through the smoke something as big as a house was seen to go down—the very earth trembled at the shock.

The smoke cleared in a moment and there lay Djek. She never moved: the round shot went clean through her body and struck the opposite wall with great force. It was wonderful, and sad, to see so huge a creature robbed of her days in a moment by a spark. There she lay—poor Djek!

In one moment I forgot all her faults. She was an old companion of mine in many a wet day and dreary night. She was reputation to me and a clear six hundred a-year—and then she was so clever. We shall never see her like again—and there she lay. I mourned over her, right or wrong, and have never been the same man since that shot was fired.

The butchery done, I was informed by the municipal authorities that the carcase was considered upon the whole to be my property. The next moment I had two hundred applications for elephant-steaks from the pinch-gut natives, who, I believe, knew gravy by tradition and romances that had come all the way from Paris : knives and scales went to work, and, with the tears running down my cheeks, I sold her beef at four sous per pound for about £40 sterling.

This done, all my occupation was gone. Geneva was no place for me, and, as the worthy Huguet, whose life I had saved, threatened to arrest me, I determined to go back to England and handicraft. Two days after Djek's death I was hanging sorrowfully

over the bridge when some one drew near to
me and said in a low voice, Mons. Loett. I
had no need to look up, I knew the voice, it
was my lost sweetheart; she spoke very
kindly, blushed and welcomed me to her
native country. She did more: she told me
she lived five miles from Geneva, and invited
me to visit her mother: she took occasion to
let me know that her father was dead: 'my
mother refuses me nothing' she added, with
another blush. This was all like a dream to
me: the next day I visited her and her
mother, and was cordially received; in short
it was made clear to me that my misfortune
had endeared me to this gem of a girl instead
of repelling her. An uncle too had died and
left her three hundred pounds, and this made
her bolder still and she did not conceal her
regard for me. She told me she had seen me
once in Geneva driving two showy horses in
a carriage and looking like a nobleman, and
so had hesitated to claim the acquaintance:

but hearing the elephant's execution, and guessing that I could no longer be on the high road to fortune she had obeyed her heart and been the first to remind me I had once esteemed her.

In short, a Pearl.

I made her a very bad return for so much goodness. I went and married her. We then compounded with Huguet for three thousand francs, and sailed for England to begin the world again.

The moment I got to London I made for the Seven Dials to see my friend Paley

On the way I meet a mutual acquaintance, told him where I was going—red hot.

He shook his head, and said nothing.

A chill came over me. If you had stuck a knife in me I shouldn't have bled. I gasped out some sort of inquiry.

'Why you know he was not a young man' says he : and he looked down.

That was enough for such an unlucky one as

me. I began to cry directly 'Don't ye take on' says he. 'Old man died happy Come home with me—my wife will tell you more about it than I can.'

I was loath to go but he persuaded me. His wife told me the old gentleman spoke of me to the last and had my letters read out and boasted of my success.

'Didn't I tell you he would rise,' he used to say, and then it seems he made much of some little presents I had sent him from Paris—and them such trifles compared with what I owed him ' doesn't forget old friends now he is at the top of the tree' and then burst out praising me by all accounts.

So then it was a little bit of comfort to think he had died while I was prosperous, and that my disappointment had never reached his warm and feeling heart.

A workman has little time to grieve outwardly; he must dry his eyes quickly let his heart be ever so sad; or he'll look queer when

Saturday night comes. You can't make a
workmanlike joint with the tear in your eye ;
one half the joiners can't do it with their
glasses on. And I was a workman once more,
I had to end as I began.

I returned to the violin trade, and, by a
very keen attention to its mysteries, I made
progress, and having a foreign connection I
imported and sold to English dealers, as well
as made, varnished, and doctored violins.
But soon the trade, through foreign competi-
tion, declined to a desperate state. I did not
despair, but to eke out, I set my wife up in a
china and curiosity shop in Wardour Street,
and worked at my own craft in the back parlour. I had no sooner done this than the
writers all made it their business to sneer at
Wardour Street, and now nobody dares buy in
that street, so since I began this tale we have
closed the shop—it only wasted their time—
they are much better out walking and getting
fresh air at least for their trouble. I attend

sales and never lose a chance of turning a penny; at home I make and mend and doctor fiddles—I carve wood—I clean pictures and gild frames. I cut out fruit and flowers in leather—I teach ladies and gentlemen to gild at so much a lesson, and by these and a score more of little petty arts I just keep the pot boiling.

I am, as I have been all my life, sober, watchful, enterprising, energetic and unlucky.

In early life I played for a great stake—affluence.

I think I may say I displayed in the service of Djek some of those qualities, by which, unless books are false, men have won campaigns and battles, and reaped fortunes and reputations—result in my case—a cannon-shot fired in a dirty little village calling itself a city, in a country that Yorkshire could eat up and spit out again, after all the great kingdoms and repubs. had admired her and forgiven her her one defect—a tongue of fire

—a puff of smoke—and the perils, labour, courage, and perseverance of eleven years blown away like dust to the four winds of heaven.

I am now playing for a smaller stake : but I am now as usual playing my very best. I am bending all my experience of work and trade, all my sobriety, activity, energy, and care, all my cunning of eye and hand, to one end—not to die in the workhouse.

Ladies and gentlemen the workman has said his say : and I hope the company have been amused.

THE END.

www.ingramcontent.com/pod-product-compliance
Lightning Source LLC
Chambersburg PA
CBHW020348030726
47496CB00007B/2054